THE BIRTH OF EMMA K.

SEAGULL
BOOKS
•
CELEBRATING
40 YEARS

THE HUNGARIAN LIST

ZSOLT LÁNG

THE BIRTH OF EMMA K.
AND OTHER STORIES

TRANSLATED BY
OWEN GOOD AND OTTILIE MULZET

LONDON NEW YORK CALCUTTA

THE HUNGARIAN LIST
Series Editor: Ottilie Mulzet

Seagull Books, 2023

Originally published in Hungarian
© Zsolt Láng, 2023

First published in English translation by Seagull Books, 2023

English translation of 'At the Western Gate' and 'The Cloister of
Sanctuary' © Ottilie Mulzet, 2023

English translation of all other stories © Owen Good, 2023

ISBN   978 0 8574 2 986 5

British Library Cataloguing-in-Publication Data
A catalogue record for this book is available from the British Library

Typeset at Seagull Books, Calcutta, India
Printed and bound in the USA by Integrated Books International

contents

GOD ON GELLÉRT HILL

Our Lord was ruminating over who gave him the power through which he created the Earth and the Sky and the living creatures from clay, from whom this boundless power came and, if it was now his own, why it wasn't absolute. Because it wasn't absolute.

Our Lord was sitting in Budapest, in Buda on Gellért Hill, or rather standing, and looking at the foggy Danube valley. That is, he wasn't looking at it, he was staring at it. With his boundless power, piercing through not only the fog but walls too, he could have caught and punished countless liars but he didn't. Instead, fixing his gaze below, he breathed a prayer to an all-powerful God, asking that Ida Pallády's mind be taken.

That Our Lord was sitting or standing about on the side of Gellért Hill, at the top of Számadó Street near the Sióvölgyi family's villa, would be an exaggeration. Our Lord doesn't tend to sit or stand about, he floats. But just so we aren't constantly searching for words and forever refining what we come up with, let's postulate that we're not talking about the Father or the Holy Ghost, we're talking about the Son, and then we can confidently say that there stood the Son of God at the corner of Számadó Street and Tündérlaki Hollow, in front of

1

the Sióvölgyi family's villa, or at least that's the name that was engraved with intricate lettering into the small nickel-plated sign on the wrought-iron gate. He was dawdling in front of the porter's cabin, which hadn't been built for a porter but the rubbish, so the bags could be locked up from bin-hokers and stray dogs who often wandered up the hill. He was waiting a short distance away from the shed because it crossed his mind that he himself might be mistaken for a bin-hoker and wind up in an altercation. He kicked his heels there for at least ten minutes and prayed as he waited, nervously staring at the town. Suddenly he gave a start and his gaze dropped towards the figure making her way up Számadó Street, none other than Ida Pallády. It was no accident then that Our Lord was loitering where he was. Nor was it any accident that he wasn't pondering the wealthy patients of the concrete alcohol rehab centre opposite or the probiotic kefir in his pocket but was utterly immersed in the problem of Ida Pallády.

Ida Pallády herself was barely known in wider circles, but her surname said a lot. Her great-grandfather was the famous pilot who was the first Hungarian to fly across the ocean. There are some of course who contest that he was Hungarian, after all, every member of the family professed to be Italian, but the point is that Guidó Pallády chose Budapest to be his home, and every one of his descendants grew up here. Ida had never set foot in Italy and spoke no languages other than Hungarian. She prays to Our Lord in Hungarian too, but so intensely that Our Lord understands, what's more, he listens readily and willingly, and as he does, he's thrown out of joint and gets caught in the eddying invocation like a fire whirl, unable to get free. Nor does he want to. Our Lord wants to help Ida.

Ida never had a religious upbringing, at most Our Lord was mentioned as a swear word, but since Ida wasn't the cursing type, she seldom said his name. But Our Lord still heard her, as he did the silent prayer of the probiotic kefir carton, in which the 250 ml carton, glued through a special process, asked Our Lord that it might hold strong against the building pressure of carbon dioxide emitted as the kefir fungi matured, and not burst at the seams. As for Ida, she prayed for things Our Lord couldn't grant because if he did, it'd cause a stir the size of which not even he could resolve. He'd tried several times to divert Ida's attention, but she was adamant.

Ida was an auditor in a nearby institute, but that's by the by, the crucial thing was that in the neighbouring office worked Tamás Simon, who Ida liked to chat with, what's more, the young man wrote poetry, and she adored poetry, so she began to adore him. Indeed the reason Ida came climbing up Számadó Street, taking advantage of her lunch break to climb Gellért Hill to the abandoned playground below the Citadel, and plumped herself on a graffitied bench, letting the gusts of wind dry her tears, was the following: three months earlier, Ida had allowed Tamás Simon to spend a long weekend at hers, what's more, she hadn't just welcomed him into her flat or into her bed but into her body too, not primarily because she would enjoy it, although she did, but because she adored him. As a result of this invitation, their lives didn't simply become entwined, they became entangled to different degrees, and consequently Tamás broke up with Ida a month ago, and, what's more, took a job offer and began working in the Pest side of the city. In his absence, Ida's adoration grew stronger, but it wasn't adoration any more, it was burning hatred. She wished Tamás would burn in Hell, that his shapely body would be torn to smithereens and that each of the thousands of little particles would suffer individually, multiplying the agony a thousand times. Our Lord tried to divert Ida's attention, going so far as to win her four numbers in the lottery worth a modest sum, then three days later in a car crash he killed her mum, or rather he called Mrs László Pallády to him, but neither the sudden stroke of luck nor the mourning snapped her out of it. She had such capacity for hate, Tamás had fled even farther and relocated to Debrecen in the east of the country, but was constantly sent back to Budapest due to his presumed contacts. Tamás did his best to wriggle out of such jobs, but quickly realized he was less anxious when he was sent than when he wasn't. He missed her, and not just her body, into which he'd been welcomed three months ago, and not just welcomed—entreated to stay, pampered, showered with everything an honoured and welcome guest would be. He admits it, he got sad because he couldn't escape the thought that this exciting sojourn would become a tedious trek, because bodies waste away and habits thrive, but he also has to admit this sadness has no grounds, it's based on blurred prejudices, whereas the current Debrecen one is true sadness, and so he's asking Ida that they pick up where they lift off and carry on with the same upward trajectory. Ida slammed the phone down, but not before yelling, fuck off and die, you pig, because she thought Tamás meant to fleece her of everything, like a robber with a blacked-out victim.

But Ida hadn't blacked out, the slam of the receiver and its disintegration in her hand attested to the contrary, not to mention the burning desire to be standing beside Tamás, to wrap the coil around his neck, and to pull it tight until his head went blue. Ida played out this strangling scene several times a day, and her muscles had grown so much from the exertion that she had to replace the cable on the office phone four times already. The image of the torn wires and their fraying ends demonstrates how potently Ida could also pray. It's little wonder Our Lord appeared at the top of Számadó Street. But that wasn't all, because walking up the adjacent Tündérlaki Hollow was none other than Tamás himself. Though he was still at the bottom, since his legs were longer than Ida's, seemingly they would arrive at the same time in front of the rehab centre on the small square, where Our Lord was also waiting.

Tamás was in love with Ida, there was no question, he fell in love at first sight. If that was the case, why did he leave her a month ago? He thought he knew why. Because through the open bathroom door he caught a glimpse of Ida washing the bath out after him, he saw her rinsing it with the showerhead, disgustedly, though he'd already done so. But it wouldn't have mattered, had she not just five minutes later slandered the Chinese with the same disgust on her pretty face: They're swarming the whole country, and they can't even learn proper Hungarian, and they smell, they can wash all they like but they'll always be dirty, and they should send their kids to their own schools, the last thing we need is them together with Hungarians, once there was a Gypsy classmate, the whole class got nits. That's what she said to him, then rolled onto him and made grand promises that come Christmas she'd have a separate gift for every inch of his body.

5

Another five minutes, three even, and they'll meet at the corner of Számadó Street and Tündérlaki Hollow. They won't be surprised because not a minute goes by when one doesn't think of the other longingly, yet still furious, desperate and angry that the other is so different. Ida Pallády hates Tamás so much that Our Lord worried the hatred would catch hold of himself too, and he'd smite the young man down in front of her with a lightning bolt. That's the last thing he wanted; the consequences of a November lightning strike were catastrophic, besides, he'd prefer to avoid that because yesterday Ida visited a fortune teller in Buda called Enikő—though her real name was Tatjana Fjodorovna, she was a Georgian refugee, more precisely, she was the fugitive wife of a Russian mafioso in Georgia, hiding out under a false name—and for a sum she had put a curse on Tamás; ergo, if he's struck by lightning now, Our Lord would be playing into the hands of some halfwit palm reader. To say nothing of picking a fight with the Russian mafia.

They met in front of Our Lord and he saw their hearts leap. Admittedly, at that moment with a wave of the hand he swept the fog away from under the Sun, and with the sudden wash of brilliance he did sneak a pinch of goodness and modesty into their hearts. Though they could hardly breathe from the shock, though warmth filled their hearts and they wanted to throw off their clothes, though they wanted to rush into one another's arms, they locked their delight away in a cage of indifference. They agreed at least to stroll to the top of Gellért Hill and have a coffee. Tamás suggested the Citadella Cafe but Ida didn't like it, so not far from the rehab clinic they sat down in a glass-walled cafe facing the hillside.

Our Lord followed them, as long as he's here, he wants to see it through to the end. There's still no guarantee he'll intervene. Creation is like throwing a stone: There's that ballistic arc from taking aim until reaching the target, and then there are the changes caused by gravity and wind; to intervene meant to retroactively meddle with time, at least that's what a philosopher claimed with whom Our Lord didn't agree (hence he never read the philosopher's thoughts, though he could see into them). Our Lord is Our Lord because he sees things differently, he thinks differently, his reasoning is different from man's. But let's not get mixed up in the difficulties of creation. The situation's already complicated enough; Tamás can't understand why four months ago he didn't even notice Ida, three months ago he was writing her poems, two months ago he was sicker of her than of her fake silk pyjamas or her colossal fridge, all the while Ida couldn't take her hands off him, whereas now he's crazy about her and she's slamming down the phone. But maybe that too will change, after all, they can only have been reunited by the indomitable will of fate. Meanwhile Ida can't understand why she's completely forgotten her rage at one stroke; why she hasn't pulled from her handbag the kitchen knife she carries everywhere so that should the opportunity arise she could slit Tamás's neck.

Our Lord listened to their conversation with innate curiosity. They were talking about Mrs Pallády's ridiculous death, about death, about loneliness, about broken fridges, about the kitsch fountain in Debrecen. Tamás ordered two shots of Unicum and two coffees from the boy in the cafe, Ida adeptly adding the kind of coffee and the quantity of milk she'd like, and most importantly that the milk was to be warm. Tamás said please and thank you—Ida didn't.

Tamás couldn't tell her what he had wanted to. He could feel how important it was but he said nothing. Not because he was afraid, but because he couldn't find the words, that is, he did tell her, of course he told her, and she asked, Why do you want to change me? I don't! So why'd you say you did? I don't, I just want to be with you. Don't bother, you're incapable, you care about no one but yourself! I do, all I care about is you. What are you talking about; you haven't even noticed my new glasses! I didn't notice because I care about you, I'm listening to you. If you cared, you'd have noticed! Come on, you've ordered a new pair of glasses identical to the old pair, just so you can say, fuck me! Fuck you! Impotent scumbag! You shit! Ponce! Slut!

Our Lord held his head in his hands. Moments before, he watched in bewilderment as a Croatian coach swept past the cafe and he recognized in one of the windows among the gawking tourists Radovan Gujevic, wanted around the globe on a charge of ethnic cleansing, nowhere to be seen, then here he is in Budapest. Even though it was a place Our Lord liked no more than other cities of the world, a second ago, while taking in the reddish-golden hillside, it did pain him a little that he hadn't seen it for so long, it was such a beautiful city, like Paris or London, but different. He was lost in his thoughts and didn't notice which one foul word between Ida and Tamás had turned their words so sour. He stamped a foot and the glass walls shook, tremors ran through the cups, the glasses and the brandy bottles on the glass shelves. Even the bar stools began to rock. Once the shelves had quietened down, the cafe boy looked out at the sky and cursed those bloody sound-barrier-breaking aeroplanes. But not a single jet plane was trailing across the sky, as the nation's military leaders were having lunch in the Golden Chalice restaurant below the Citadella, with the air marshals of the British Royal Air Force; it would've been improper to disturb the officers with a sonic boom, besides, the planes weren't to escort the guest aircraft back to the border for another two hours yet. The couple fell silent and hadn't the energy to go on. Tamás decided he was better off without Ida; in hopeless longing, Ida also thought how good it'd be to go home alone, throw herself on the bed and sob away her pain, and afterwards to carry on hating, tearing apart the phone cable and gripping at the wooden handle of the kitchen knife.

Except that Our Lord didn't want it to end like that. Especially as he was there. The best would be, he thought, if the Croatian coach, not the one hiding Gujevic but the next, were to drive into the glass-walled cafe because of a leak in the brake fluid, and the guests inside would be gathered up in pieces, and the police wouldn't even know how many had met their deaths; then the owner of the cafe who'd been dreaming of a new life for a while now would seize the opportunity to go to Australia and live in a fishing village until the day he died, happy because nobody ever asked where he was from. But Our Lord didn't have the power. Anyway, he didn't want Ida or Tamás to die. With these two he wanted to send a message to those he created in his own image. An important message. Maybe, if Ida was to fall pregnant, and when the child grew up if it discovered and understood life's greatest secret. Or maybe if it had some special ability. Like it could fly. Or at least walk on water.

He let out a weary sigh. He fell to his knees. He didn't care any more. He'd grown tired of bearing the endless cross of not-quite-absolute power. They took no notice that he was even there. Even if the agony drove them into the ground, they still wouldn't change an iota. Ida would never move her fridge an inch so that Tamás wouldn't bump his elbow when he entered the kitchen from the bathroom. Tamás would never drop his accusatory tutting. No, these two were incapable of rising above it and looking down on the certainty of their own existence. The agony of such a life would drive him into the ground. The agony of his own was already driving him into the ground. The next time he was endowed with power, he wanted it to be absolute. There was no point otherwise. A stone throw is perfect only when the fist doesn't let go but flies with the stone.

Translated by Owen Good

DAPHNE

1

On the afternoon before the trip, I met Klára at Pallas Bookshop. The rain started as a drizzle and grew heavier: How about a coffee in Melody Caffé? Luckily it was packed. On our way out, she told me her parrot had died and asked me to help her bury it. I held the door for her and paused a while, staring at her quivering backside. She was wearing trendy, yellow silk trousers and no underwear. I marvelled at how desire could just vanish, without a trace. As though it had been sucked out of me by some sort of spidery, hairy beastie— slurp!

The rain stopped and we were heading towards the Philharmonic. I noticed the darkness of the tan on her neck. It was hideous but she obviously thought the bronze suited her. She tied her hair up in a bun and put in some shell-shaped clips. She was trying to bowl me over, she waited for me to catch up:

'Have you been on holiday?'

'Not yet.'

'When are you going?'

'Tomorrow.'

'Where to?'

'Rome.'

'You've been there.'

'I know.'

'You've been thinking about it.'

'I have.'

'Me too, those spectacular . . .'

I didn't let her go into raptures, I curtly took my leave and headed off towards the puppet theatre. She called after me.

'Will you help me?'

'With?'

'Who'll bury Marci?'

'Feed him to the cat.'

2

It'd been a turbulent time for us, I was tired and my ears rang constantly. I would have gone mad in a quiet artist's residency in the hills. Rome came just in time, and the never-ending traffic of Via Giulia and Sangallo.

I didn't take the metro out to Ostia, even though for the first day I'd planned to swim in the sea and have dinner on Campo. I'd been put off the beach thanks to Klára. I could see her in front of me scorching in the sun like some kind of maniac.

So I was in Rome, cutting across Navona as I hurried to the Spanish Steps. I jogged across the busy Corso and soon came to a small triangular square on the narrow Via delle Mercede. It must have been barely nine in the morning, yet there were droves of people milling about on the streets with grave, stony expressions. The faces only softened in the evening when darkness settled on the city until even those up on the viewpoints or in the windows saw nothing.

I noticed that the woman approaching me along the narrow Via delle Mercede was stroking her bare stomach. She pushed the bottom hem of her strapless top up to her nipple so unabashedly and unashamedly that my breath caught in my throat. I cast a curious glance at her face but found no explanation. In her other hand she held a shopping bag and from her shoulder there hung a black patent-leather bag. Red lines and bruises shone on her stomach, and glancing up again, I saw more on her face.

Somehow she was prompting me to some sort of action, like Klára had, two days before, strolling towards the Philharmonic. Except now I didn't want to get away, on the contrary, I spoke to her:

'Can I help you?'

She didn't answer, but seemed to signal with her elbow to wait, then came next to me and with her left arm, the one she'd been stroking her chest with, she linked into mine. She didn't stop, she swept me onwards.

Though her body was extremely fragile, she was the one leading. We've melded together like two drops of water, I thought. In my head I'd prepared a muddled monologue about why I'd come to Rome. I'm not a tourist and I'm not a pilgrim, although I do want to find the places I visited last year . . .

I don't have a clue why I'm here . . . This city calls to me . . . I want to stay forever . . . I'd like to be built into the wall of a house or erected under a balcony. I mean . . .

Before I could even speak, we were on Navona, cutting through the African sellers and their handbags, past the Bernini fountain and the church of Sant'Agnese, and in the alleyway beside the Nardecchia, we suddenly came to the door of an ancient building. She lived there on the top floor.

The second we entered, the lights automatically came on and light filled the rooms. She still hadn't said a word. Not that conversation was lacking but I was curious for some kind of explanation. She collapsed on the bed and closed her eyes, and I, in the meantime, just stood there full of questions.

I took a tour of the flat, stopping here and there in front of open cupboards, paintings and photographs hanging on the walls. I moved comfortably, like going through an old favourite score of music. I made coffee, nibbled on a few biscuits and settled myself in a cool armchair.

I had risen early that day because I planned on catching the deserted peace at dawn, but I was disappointed; there were marauding groups of tourists everywhere. The rolling hills of Rome had simply been flattened under the tireless feet, the creases had been smoothed out, the cool valleys had disappeared . . . On Piazza San Pietro there were as many elated throngs as had once been in the circus that stood there long ago. I escaped along Via dei Corridori, staring longingly at curtained windows.

An eager beggar pounced on me in front of Castel Sant'Angelo. He had dirty, dark wadding in his ears.

'Spare something, sir?'

'No.'

'Spare change, I'm hungry.'

'If you'd asked for some bread . . .'

'I'll take bread.'

'Would you?'

'A bite.'

'Drop by my place, I'll give you some.'

'I'll come with you.'

'I'm not going home now. Let's say in an hour in front of 68 Via Giulia.'

'Are you screwing with me? That's the juvenile prison, I know it.'

'I live beside it. I'll leave it in a bag on the bench there.'

'They'll think it's a bomb, there's police all over.'

'Okay, I'll be there, you wait on the bench.'

The sleeping woman's spacious flat was calming, with its photos on the walls of Indigenous Americans smiling back at me. Since running away from Klára I was feeling more cheerful by the hour. For a long time I could only see the image of her backside quivering in the silk trousers and could no longer stifle the laughter tickling at my sides. Klára was a victim of fashion . . . While I complimented her at least three times daily: You look stunning! I laughed at the thought of my cowardice. But forget that, let's not stray beyond the beginning of the story. My trip promised to be a happy one. On the train in Vienna some Japanese girls were sitting in my cabin, chatting constantly, munching on chocolate Neapolitan wafers, and there's nothing more enjoyable than Japanese student girls muttering away, mouths full of wafers. I sat back with a smile and stared contentedly out the window at the farmland along the Po, as though my own granaries were swelling with the harvested yield. People who visit Rome a second time imagine themselves to be globetrotters and are willing to embark on bold adventures. Right there on the train I decided to quit the orchestra and go solo, despite the fact that our audience didn't like unusual acts. I still shudder at the thought of the icy obstinacy with which the world-famous Yevtushenko was received when, holding a Steinway fallboard, he introduced La Monte Young's classic 'Piano Piece' . . . I had to explain the meaning of the spectacle to Klára too. What is music? Music is the creative shaping of auditory matter which, as a part of nature and an expression of impulse, represents the world and the soul in the auditory domain with incomprehensible accuracy . . . Klára was serious, like the companion to music.

I had broken free from the shackles of a relationship, arrived in the capital of the world, escaped a beggar and, of course, I was resting in the shade beside a sleeping woman who, on the face of it, had an affiliation to no one but myself. In front of me I saw a classic beauty skirted in anonymity. The one snag was she'd been beaten. The bruises hung over her beautiful body like clouds of black smog.

Perhaps she'll sleep it off by the evening, I thought, nodding off. But she didn't come around until the next morning.

3

She was called Daphne, but her Indigenous name was Nonni, meaning spring raindrop. She wasn't Indigenous, she just married a Peruvian; he was a painter, and he was always painting her . . . Then her husband and her four-year-old boy were hit by a timber lorry. The dumper had wheels the size of two full-grown men . . . She can't talk about that any more. She lived in Peru for eleven years, Mexico for seven, and then flew back. She left at sixteen, when she was called back, she was thirty-four.

'Who called you back?'

'Fabio.'

'Who's Fabio?'

'Don't ask.'

'Is he the one that beat you?'

'You know the San Giorgio? He blew it up.'

'He blew up a church?'

'It's where the Greeks went. They were a problem.'

'What do you mean?'

'Don't ask.'

'And the Greeks?'

'They fixed the church and went after Fabio.'

'Did they get him?'

'Fabio wanted to sweet-talk them. He used me.'

'Christ, Nonni, I don't want to know. I mean, go on.'

'Help me, please!'

'Of course, I'll help you.'

Fabio didn't believe that Nonni wanted out. Why bother, he said, she'll be back after three days, begging to get back in. He won't go looking for her. Anyway, the Olympics is on.

The Olympics started the day I arrived, 13 August. I knew that because when I was choosing the dates I hoped everyone would be flying to Athens, so Rome would be completely empty.

Nonni woke up at dawn when the day was barely breaking, then fell asleep again as the sun came up. Myself, half-asleep, I listened to her stories from Peru, until slowly I came around, and when my head had cleared, she stopped and detailed the things I was to buy and where. I went out and got everything, meanwhile stopping here and there to look around, I was in Rome after all. I picked up a load of postcards. I thought of sending one to Klára, then thought better of it, in case she drew the wrong conclusion. She thinks there's an immense mother complex at work inside me, hence she claimed the right to treat me like a child. I've no idea whether I have a mother complex, but with Klára I did act like a child. At the last rehearsal of the season I soaped up her strings. Poor Klára! During the practice the conductor yelled at her, little lady, are you trying to play a violin or beat a cock?! The whole room fell apart laughing. I, of course, bit my tongue, I could've told them she plays the latter with such finesse she might be following a score.

Nonni was obsessed with getting some butter and asked me to buy it in bulk. She sent me all the way out to Testaccio Market because it was the only place to get Burro Siciliano by the kilo. She laid out a map under the floor lamp and showed me where to go. Remember, she told me, the market's pretty small, plus I wasn't looking for the main market but a row of stalls next to it on Via Bodini. The next time, she just peevishly gave the order, where to go and what to get, without putting me right on the map. When I got back, she woke up and anxiously asked whether I'd found the place.

'Nonni, what do you need with all this butter?'

'I got used to it.'

'You don't eat.'

'They eat a lot of butter in Peru.'

'I'm sure.'

'That's why they live so long.'

'That's the climate. Like your phone lasts longer if the signal's good.'

'Butter's a medicine there.'

'Then let's butter your wounds.'

'They don't hurt.'

She didn't complain, but I could see she wasn't in a good way. The bruises had turned green and the centres black, they stared at me like horrific eyes. Often she shivered so much from the cold that she couldn't speak. She held my arm as she fell asleep.

4

On the third day I picked up my things. I cancelled my previous accommodation and moved into hers. My reasoning being if I was receiving free lodging and free food, I could buy a few soon-to-be-rare records. I spent whole mornings in the Argentinian record shop. Then I got bored of that too. The city was a torrent of sensations, and I had no one to share it with. Nonni didn't care what I'd seen, just like she didn't care where I was from, or what I did.

'It's that kind of city.'

'What kind?'

'It doesn't let you speak.'

'What do you mean?'

'Only it can speak.'

'You're right.'

'It crushes you.'

'It does!'

'Of course.'

'Uh-huh.'

I talked matters over with myself, but our thoughts were too uniform and our conversation soon died out. There were other failures. One evening I went out to the Theatre of Marcellus where an English pianist happened to be playing a concert; I listened from the top row, sitting under the wall. Beside me was a local in a vest flicking through a car magazine. I could see he wasn't interested in the music. Indeed the programme wasn't the best, so I greeted him in a friendly manner. Nothing. I tried again, doing my utmost to make my pronunciation of each syllable as Italian as possible. At which he glanced up amusedly, then looked right through me like I was air, lifted one buttock, and let out a parp. I entered Sant'Ignazio Church where the ceiling's fresco staggered me, leaving me dumbstruck. I crossed the space to my boyhood-favourite Saint Anthony, certain he'd understand but saw he stood almost buried under a mountain of letters and realized he wouldn't have time to talk either. I wanted to ask a priest what he'd recommend—he didn't wait for me to finish and mechanically directed me to a long queue. There were at least fifty people in front of me inching towards the distant confessional booth . . . It's that kind of city . . .

Next to the Tiber, I left the jogging track and descended to the riverside. One angler, as far as the eye could see.

'Catch anything?'

'Last time there was a painting caught on my hook.'

'A painting?'

'The frame was worth a fortune.'

'You sold it?'

'Got five hundred for it.'

'Euros?'

'What else? But as long as we're chatting, will you take over while I get a bottle of water?'

I waited for him until late in the day to no avail. It was near dark when I packed up and went home. In the morning I went down again in case the rod's owner appeared. I'd never seen a fishing rod so big, it was at least ten metres long, and on the end was a vice-like contraption as thick as a man's arm. Seeing as I was there already, I got stuck into the fishing. The tramps living further down at the Cloaca Maxima came over to marvel and took the fish gratefully. When I cast the hook and the lure, I merely had to think of Nonni and something bit, the float was sunk.

I brought some for Nonni but she didn't like fish.

'Why won't you eat?'

'I can't chew.'

'I'll chew it for you.'

'I can't swallow.'

'I'll swallow it for you.'

'I'm going blind.'

Her condition was getting worse. She was constantly shivering but she threw the cover off herself. When she fell silent for a few minutes, her thin body became translucent, to the point where I could see the moving dark shadows of her lungs. Her nostrils turned transparent as well, as though her nose was about to drip. I was constantly reaching for a tissue to wipe it . . .

5

I spread the butter thick over the bread so she'd put on weight. The light spun in strange circles in front of me, even when I closed my eyes—in fact, that's when it was worst. It was as though I could see through my eyelids.

'It's a lack of sleep.'

'What should I do?'

'Get away for a while.'

'All right. I will. Where?'

'Naples.'

'Okay.'

'Leave right away.'

'Nonni's here . . .'

'She'll sleep it off.'

'She's getting worse.'

'You can't help that.'

'Maybe she really is longing for Fabio.'

'Hard luck.'

'If it weren't for this Fabio . . .'

'You two would lead a quiet little life here.'

'Like two old friends.'

One time I said to Nonni, shouldn't I tell Fabio not to worry about her any more, the three days were long up. Horrified, she cried and cried for hours. I had to swear on my mother's life I wouldn't. I pulled her close to comfort her. Stroking her body, I tried to waken some form of desire in her but got nowhere.

I suddenly remembered the beggar. First Klára and then the beggar. Klára's slow, stupid body, her selfishness that rendered me as defenceless as a beggar, the selfishness that I drew out of her so that should she come to her senses, she would have to give me something. Hence the beggar. Perhaps he was still waiting for me on Via Giulia. The butter had begun to smell—I thought I'd bring him some. I packed it in a plastic bag.

I traipsed the route from the 64 Bus Stop to the Spada several times before taking a seat on the bench. I waited. Later the sun emerging from behind the buildings began to burn, and I escaped into the Criminology Museum.

The museum's artefacts were exhibited on the corridors and bays of the Ministry of Justice. On one side, a secretary chattered about her Granny's snoring, on the other, in a display case, there lay a sharpened tuning fork: the weapon used to stab one of the Pope Urbans to death. There was a row of dainty guillotines, and hanging on the wall were imitation paintings, most of them outstandingly poor. I came across funnier objects too, the matronly pair of high-waisted knickers upon which Antonio Missi, the designer of the infamous Bologna bank robbery, wrote a confession of his love to his sweetheart with a burnt match. Beside them was a Smena camera belonging to a Hungarian female spy, Bernadett Varga, born in a nonexistent misspelt town in Hungary, and which she'd used to photograph NATO documents in the Florence library. And naturally there were countless rifles and pistols, artefacts of the Mafia's seized arsenal. The timer that was used to blow up San Giorgio Church, that is, an exact copy that had randomly malfunctioned. And a photo of the accused Fabio Negri, beside a picture of the entire notorious Negri family—the glorious congregation—at least four generations; from which it was clear that the inheritance passing from father to son wasn't restricted to the tools of the trade, flick knives and concealed sleeve pistols, but also the characteristically huge Negri ears: Fabio bore a pair, as did his little brother, the black sheep of the family who ventured off to the Red Brigades, Tonio.

By the time I left, the butter was dripping from the bag and a lean dog was licking it off the bench. My leg was shaking and I headed into the Orphans' Church. I made an attempt at the Lord's Prayer but Fabio's face burst into my mind and I shook with laughter. Jug-ears Fabio! And I just laughed.

'How've you ended up here with this lot?'

'I've no idea.'

'Leave them!'

'Obviously.'

'Leave the whole shebang behind.'

'I'm going to Naples. For a week. Or two.'

'What'll Klára say when you don't come back!'

'The quartet's everything to her. I'm leaving it anyway.'

'Just right!'

'She wears white tights with black silk dresses . . .'

'And the earrings!'

'The clips . . .'

'Get yourself to the station this minute, forget your bags.'

'Of course. It's only a small suitcase, no loss.'

'You've enough money.'

'Small but practical.'

'Two pairs of trousers, three shirts, you'll get new ones.'

'The records. The Toscaninis!'

'Oh, and the Schuberts.'

'Why leave them?'

'True.'

'Old jug-ears would toss them out.'

'He's only interested in the Olympics.'

'Maybe they're over . . .'

'They are.'

6

When I got home, I was met by something unexpected: Nonni was up. I asked whether she felt better and she nodded. But she walked around the room like she was about to collapse. She couldn't manage to walk from the kitchen to the bathroom,

I had to help her. She was as thin as a rake. I wrapped one arm around her and lifted her on my hip. The thought being I'd carry her in my arms, perhaps it agitated her but I found the act soothing. She threw up a white liquid, long, glistening strings hung from her mouth. She whimpered.

'You have to get butter.'

She sent me to the Trastevere on the most winding route yet. I had to ask for Vittorio beside the flea market. He lived in a narrow, two-storey building with the pizzeria under his room. His customers watched him work as they stood at the sidebars along the walls and stuffed food in their mouths with their bare hands. I should ask him for a block of butter, but only the best. I'm to pay him with a medallion dangling on a gold chain because then he'll know who sent me.

I found it odd, or I didn't find it odd because I'd got used to Nonni's eyes. I crossed the scorching Ponte Sisto with determination and continued along the nicer side of the Tiber, under the plane trees until San Gallicano. Other than the Senegalese embassy, there's no building in Rome more dilapidated. I wandered along the narrow Via del Moro until Dante's house, from there down the stairs covered in dog shit until Piazza di San Cosimato, because Nonni, whenever possible, always sent me via stairways. They keep you on your toes! Meanwhile I had to go into the Santa Cecilia Church but I couldn't stay long, I hurried along the wall of the Mint until the Franciscans and to the back of the flea market.

Night falls early in Rome, earlier than at home. But slowly, over at least three hours and the light changes dramatically. It lifts the veil on secrets, but in such a way that the secret is still ominous. Once a scarlet-faced German conductor called our attention to the fact that there was no first note to the Creation, since the first note was the second on the scale: 're', in other words, Haydn keeps the secret too. Last year I hadn't even noticed the cut on Santa Cecilia's neck. Or the agony on Santa Ludovica's face. These discoveries seemed like singular moments, but it distressed me that they could repeat themselves at any time. They forced open a fissure in front of me, a fissure I couldn't bear to look into.

Vittorio was still having his siesta up in his room. I had to knock for a while. A tired, hairy-chested bloke opened the door.

'The fuck do you want?'

'Nonni sent me. She wants your help, she's not in a good way.'

'I don't know any Nonni.'

'Her real name's Daphne, she sent this.'

He disappeared with the medallion and shortly reappeared, shoving a pack of butter in my hand, with green writing across it: 'Burro Americano'.

On the way back I followed an even more zigzagging route. Out of the Senegalese embassy came at least two dozen Black people, a mix of adults, children, men and women. I marvelled at how so many people could fit into that shack.

I'd reached Sisto Bridge when in front of the iron railings I almost bumped into who else but our good friend George. He was one of the most successful of those who'd switched careers. George Kőrössi. He'd put down the violin and become a singer, he visited cities all around the world. He performed in villages too, in Germany of course where villages are quite different from our own, so he was a rare chap, despite not being able to hit a high C unless it was transposed.

George Kőrössi, or Gyuri originally, but whose father, poor old Pista, the best cabinet maker in the town who now forges renaissance wardrobes, even called him by his English name, 'Zsorzs'.

'Look who it is.'

'I'm singing in a guesthouse in Ostia full of German tourists. But after, I'm off to the Vatican. You?'

'I'm just looking about.'

'You have to visit the Jesuit church beside the Caracalla baths, the papal ambassadors hang about there all the time, it's worth meeting them.'

'Well I'd be happy to introduce you to Daphne, come over, if you like.'

'Who?'

'She's an influential woman, knows Signor Fabio.'

'I've nothing on tonight. Give me a place and a time. Though I know the Italians don't appreciate punctuality.'

'It'll just be us and her, that's always the best.'

His face beamed. We said goodbye and he dashed up to Gianicolo to change. Supposedly his wife had bought him an unbelievably colourful silk shirt, but whether or not he was actually married was anybody's guess. There was a sort of boyish charm in the way he bounded past people. If he was ever invited somewhere, he always sat beside the most influential guest; for which he had a fantastic eye, or elbow. He spoke the language of women beautifully, performing opera librettos with long, winding flourishes and broad gestures.

7

Nonni virtually tore the butter from my hands. She broke it in two and removed something from it without showing me and ran with it into the bathroom.

I was surprised when she reappeared a while later. She was triumphant and cheerful like a musical clown. I eyed her up and down, dumbfounded, I didn't know what to think, when suddenly the bell rang and George arrived.

At first sight, our guest was stuck on Nonni. I didn't mind, apart from the fact that she left for the bathroom several times while I was left alone with a fired-up George, who was nervously drumming his fingers on his knees, until suddenly he sprung up, made for the bathroom and froze in the doorway, absentmindedly swinging his body left and right.

Around midnight I noticed the problem: Nonni's eyes were glimmering like two dark holes. Panic took over, as though I had missed the train. Or I was standing on the edge of a deep pit. I would have dashed off without so much as a word, but I stood up coolly and quietly excused myself. No one noticed.

I'd packed up my things within minutes. In the hallway I mechanically patted my pockets a second time, I had everything. I cautiously peeked back through the crack in the door: I saw Nonni already sitting in George's lap listening to *Parsifal*, though it was clear she wasn't following the story. Yet George was in his element, nodding like a duck, depicting the characters' contours with his left hand, or maybe exaggeratedly tangling the threads of the story. His gaze was lost in the distance, but upon noticing me with a chance turn of his head something struck him, because for an instant, without stopping the story, he froze in terror.

For safety's sake I wandered around the neighbourhood for hours, never taking my gaze from the house entrance. Only when the clock at Sant'Agnese struck seven did I cut across the Navona for the bus stop. The bag sellers appeared around the fountain, their black skulls shone like the paving on the square.

I took the 64 out to the station. The fermatas came ever more frequently, like in Schubert's last piano sonata. I was fretting but we arrived in time. Moreover, after I'd collected my reservation, I had enough time to take a seat in the elegant Diocletianus Pizzeria, and ordered a Carciofi alla giudea with a glass of Castelli Romani. I'm here now, no need to rush.

I could have had two glasses because the Naples train arrived twenty minutes late. Even after it rolled in and I found my seat, we wasted at least another forty. Supposedly something had happened with the engine. The Austrian ticket collector fretfully paced up and down the aisle in his terribly squeaky brown sandals. The squeaking grew higher and higher, from which I could tell he too was becoming more and more agitated because he hadn't any information either about the cause of the delay. I tipped my forehead against the window and began daydreaming about all kinds of mysterious happenings. Yes, admittedly, I wouldn't have minded, had masked men hijacked the train and taken us hostage, only to find myself in an unknown African country when I woke up.

Translated by Owen Good

CHESTNUT

My name's Gyémánt, Doctor Gyémánt, Doctor Károly Gyémánt, he would begin, were he to write this story in the first person. *Doctor Diamond* in English. If possible he'd skip the Christian name, Károly, *Charles*. Perhaps the English could be bearable, the German too, unless teetering behind the name is a barely five-foot-two dwarf, even *Karl* is pretty amusing. *Wee Charlie!*

But then names aren't everything. Is Doctor Kálmán Padlutka any more fortunate? Size doesn't matter either, of course. Yet Károly had other issues too. Beauty had been a guest to his face as a boy only, before some manner of bill was settled, and a fretful beauty sped off in search of new lodgings.

Then came something else. At first he didn't know what it was, a general malaise hinted that something was on its way, lying in wait, like jaundice or measles. But that something was already flourishing in all its glory and wafting its scent. One late summer's night, when nightmares of the approaching school year had taken over from sweet daydreams, he located the malaise's source: foot odour! He couldn't sleep. When he covered his feet, the odour seeped out from under the duvet; when he stuffed his head under the duvet, leaving his feet out, the mere memory of the odour tormented him. Out in the kitchen, his parents were arguing bitterly, unable to understand why he was so exasperated. Neither had foot odour and so their sympathy was lacking. From that summer's night onward, the unmistakeable odour took up residence in Károly's nose, or arguably directly in his brain. He washed, scrubbed, lathered and soaked his feet, but he couldn't rinse out his skull. Beyond the age of twelve, all that grew were his ears, yet somehow he'd lost every last ounce of his former self. His parents divorced.

He became a doctor, and not a bad one either. Once, for example, a fifty-eight-year-old man came to see him who'd had frequent headaches for twenty years, reaching unbearable extremes about three times a week. So he told the man to go and have a swig of whiskey. He hadn't a clue himself why he recommended this, and the man stammered in shock, he doesn't drink, he doesn't know if he should . . . Fine, cut in Károly, a half will do. And that was that, it turned out to be enough, after an hour the man returned and flew in cheerfully: his pain had disappeared. From then on, he visited once a month, steadily happier, then once a year, and now thirteen years have passed and still no headaches.

Maybe this event opened Károly's eyes as to where his real place was. He joined the reawakening homeopathic movement. He was invited evermore frequently to various conferences, and as a bachelor he was happy to travel. From time to time he was on TV. I've seen you somewhere before, hotel receptionists would say, and hand him the key reserved for those with clout; a south-facing suite with balcony and sauna, well, assuming it was that class of hotel. Unfortunately, the participants of this latest conference in Pécs were put up in a different class. What's more, one that couldn't even offer single rooms. And since for the first time in years—perhaps due to the glorious October weekend—everyone invited had actually turned up, not a single bed was vacant. Men with men, women with women, that was the grinning receptionist's policy, who couldn't help cracking a timely gag.

Károly's roomate was Albert.

Albert was quite an unusual name, but in Transylvania, where he was born, it was fairly common. His nickname was Bertsy, although at work he was strictly known as Doctor Józsa. He was a composed, visibly intelligent man, a tad conceited, a tad superficial, but a big name in his field. The two men stood in the small twin bedroom motionless.

Repulsion spread across their faces at the mere sound of the other's name. Both felt a lingering nausea. When one made his way to the microphone to give his presentation, the other left the room. Not in protest, but as if the lavatory was calling.

There was room for increasing the number of hotels in Pécs, an attentive stroll around the main square could attest to that. Albert and Károly concluded the same after both swiftly left the room and regained composure outside, breathing in the fresh air. They'd known each other since university, or earlier, since military service. They were enrolled at the same barracks, the same company, the same platoon, but the real issue was the bunk bed, with Károly in the bottom, and Albert in top. For six months straight. And on the very first night Károly's foot odour stole into Albert's brain where like some sort of powerful enzyme it produced acids of loathing and hatred. Or alkalis perhaps but the effect was the same corrosive pain which induced—besides the psychological torture—a range of abnormalities. Abnormalities which altered Albert's body to perfection, like an angelic counterpart to the caricature tossing and turning beneath him. Before enrolling he was a thin, stooping teenager, and after just six months a glowing, strapping demigod appeared before the civilians' eyes. He was like the brilliant crown of a silver birch in the summer sun, nourishing on the juices of the hideous, stinking body beneath; absorbing the sun's rays, the warm rains, and all the sublimity of the azure. Hence maybe Károly began to bear a grudge; the other's presence had become unbearable due to this unfair appointment of bunks. In the godlike visage living above, he caught a glimpse of his own deformity and felt a pathetic vulnerability in his own weakness; he had let his own life-giving substance be sucked out by the verdant bole above.

For thirty years they had avoided each other. After a while they forgot each other's names. But as they stood paralysed in the middle of their shared room, the thirty years of repressed hatred came gushing out. It couldn't even be called hatred any more, it was so lacking in form. More matter than form. Pure abhorrence.

Both leapt for the door, and nearly got jammed in the doorframe. Károly slid out first and Albert behind him. Trembling, in complete silence, they staggered down the stairs, knocking into one another again at the exit. They came out onto the square, one of them went right, the other left. The acids or alkalis corroding their brains. Memories churning in their heads, they became nauseous and had to sit on benches in the little square in front of the mosque. And what did they see? At first they thought it was a fantasy of their repulsion, but they gradually realized that sitting opposite them was the author of their sickness. They fixed their eyes on one another. They were homeopathists, homoeopathic doctors who had experimented on themselves with all sorts. So now, instinctively applying homoeopathic practice, both tried to extract a balm for their ailments from the sight of the other.

And that's when Doctor Mónika appeared, who had been dropped off by a car in the underground car park and was searching for familiar faces. The straps on her rucksack nicely contoured her round breasts. She was happy to find Károly and sat herself down beside him. When she noticed Albert on the opposite side, she suggested quite enthusiastically that they all go and have a drink, since they still had a few hours until the afternoon kick-off and she, for one, needed a drink after that trek. Hesitating first, Károly agreed in the end, and they walked over to Albert. After wandering for half an hour, with Mónika positioned between them, they sat in an empty garden bar in the chestnut grove below the cathedral and ordered three glasses of lager.

We could go on in this banal but well-oiled, soap-opera style, because the external events aren't important, rather it's the invisible line of force of the internal happenings that guides the threads woven from these sentences into a new pattern. The minutes passed slowly. That is, the hours ticked by to the usual rhythm but the mass of corrosive liquid forming in the brain soon filled the skull's capacity and could go no further. Molecular transformation set in motion. More precisely, the following events occurred: molecules split, atoms broke loose, which then too lost integrity and split into many parts, again and again. An utterly boundless energy of unnamed properties was released in the fission; the lines of force had tied in knots. And of course more things beyond these must have shifted too.

The two men didn't make eye contact, they sat paralysed, clutching at their glasses. Mónika recounted her hitchhiking adventure in great detail, deciphering the glow in the men's eyes as keyed-up interest. Which struck her. Simply because people rarely paid her any attention. She lived her life in a bit of a dream, her attention frequently strayed, she wore an expression of languid, feline boredom that frightened her colleagues, who were only ever looking for either a one-night stand or a lifelong hard-working wife. Nor was she the best suited for homoeopathy because she was forever sceptical. Patients who visited her surgery with a medical complaint left with fresh fears. She laid bare the complexity of the question, she illustrated the uncertainties of science, the brutality of our ungodly, savage world and lacked the patience to trace the tremors of the soul; in short, she approached everything from the point of view of the agnostic universe. Her tousled blonde hair hung across her forehead. She had a slight squint, only mildly but enough to unsettle pretty much anyone who tried to make eye contact. In all likelihood her squint was caused by real hurt. But no one would get past her eyes, recognize her endless traumas in their dreadful entirety, and relive those traumas in a safe space, skimming off their morals. Unfortunately, nor will the scope of the narrative allow us to cross through this coincidentally opportune passage into some wonderful story in which we might unearth the long-sought catharsis from beneath the crusts of secret love.

Hair of the dog! Albert gulped down the beer and the familiar foot odour. When he finished, he gave a stifled belch and once again the odour flooded his internal organs. Subtly he turned away from Mónika and his gaze hung on Károly's cabbage-leaf ear. He followed the dark tangle of veins on the lobe and searched the entrance to his ear for the dark hairs. Nothing had changed! He almost fainted. The distant voices echoed about him dully and fell silent, as if his head had been stuffed with cotton wool. He set down his beer and instinctively reached for his medicine. Now, yes, he ought to touch, more, to bite, to loathingly taste this heap of shit! And just the thought of the taste made him feel better. He turned back to Mónika with a smile, as she recounted the male Mazda driver's advances.

Károly followed the Mazda's journey for a while, chiefly as he was unexpectedly enlightened about the new bridge at Baja, where he would be going the next day to get to his relatives in Kiskőrös, but soon he couldn't keep his attention in a neutral state. He pictured Albert in the Mazda driver's place and almost immediately slugged him. Don't you touch her thigh, you pig! Which was a surprising reaction given he wanted nothing from Mónika, who somehow felt like a close female relative, a sister or a daughter—yet frankly he can't have been familiar with the feeling, having neither a sister nor a daughter. His body filled with fear, yes, that's the word, or almost; the kind of fear an approaching thunderstorm might cause in a walker. Though there wasn't a cloud in the sky, to his horror he saw the steely cumulation in the distance, bolts of lightning hurtling down like rockets, striking down everything in its path, living or dead. Just like in the barracks, the blossoming body sprawled above him, there arched over him the leaden vaulting, shutting off the air above him without a hope of breaking free or taking one step towards freedom, because any minute the lack of air would give him a stroke and he'd be paralysed forever. Meanwhile a voice in the distance whispered in his ear (the things he heard!), there's still a chance, he could still move, don't think, get up, jump him, batter that stinking fop into the ground! Of course, we've no means to look into his actual thoughts. He was a practician of homoeopathy, a research fellow of the fundamental energies of life-enriching matter, a scholar and student of the interchangeable fundamentals of healing; one can imagine what was going on in his head. Crush him, destroy him, rip him apart and tear him to pieces until there's not a shred of him left. Then stop your wounds with his ashes.

In that rare moment, across the vast sky of Europe there wasn't a single cloud in sight, not even with the most sensitive radars. The Mazda driver had just suggested to Mónika that they pull over and make good use of the honey-warm October morning, take a dip in the Danube, when something dropped from the sky. A single chestnut. At the very top of the tree, it popped from its split burr and plummeted, determined, towards Károly's head. The strike met the left upper suture of his skull, and the waves of resonance that were roused in the skull's plates amplified the strength of the knock, shocking the perplex neural pathway and inducing instant fainting.

Károly's face hit the table.

Heart attack! screamed Doctor Mónika. She searched for Károly's pulse, trying to resuscitate him without success, she wasn't experienced and Albert's lack of action was bothering her. You were a cardiologist, sir, do something! she shouted desperately, addressing her old teacher formally in the excitement.

Albert really had been a heart specialist. It was in the nearby Pécs heart clinic he'd started upon and reached his most spectacular results. He was capable of anything, even world-sensational transplants. He performed bypasses with his eyes closed, feeling for the veins with his naked fingers through the tiniest of incisions. Ten years ago he'd given up, stating as a justification that his much-admired manual dexterity had become rusty. While his colleagues continue to wonder about this decision, let's guess at the real reason. One of his patients refused to go under the knife though it seemed the only solution. They quarrelled. Months later he heard his patient was cured by homoeopathic treatment, from none other than Doctor Gyémánt. I'm glad I didn't listen to you, said the patient, his friend, and topped it off by calling him a butcher, a dense, bloodthirsty butcher. The news upset Albert. His face was red as he hung up the phone. And as he lifted his hand to wipe away the pearly beads of sweat from his brow, he noticed the tremor. Yes, it was mild, but it didn't go away, not that day or the next . . . And in his right hand! Perhaps it was his subconscious and revenge that drove him to homoeopathy. Or the simple command of salvation. He got a degree in Germany, worked there a few years and rapidly became so popular that the success put an end to the tremor in his hand. But by that point he would never return to the operating theatre.

They took Károly to the hospital by taxi in a ten-year-old, butter-gold Mercedes. The driver gave a hand hauling Károly into the back seat, although he didn't like lifting things due to his sensitive kidney. Albert didn't help and sat in the front seat. Once they got going, he nervously wound down the window at which the driver almost whacked his hand: air-con! He was forced to sink again into the healing waves of overdose. He thought of Károly's heart, he imagined it struggling, twitching, and choking inside. He imagined the scalpel in his hand as he made an incision in the rattling chest. A stench floods the theatre, and the staff grimace. He reaches inside, feels for the thick, clotted aorta and follows it to the heart, which is weirdly somewhere below the diaphragm, directly behind the stomach. He finds it, reaches under it and lifts it out to see its condition. He's never seen such a foul thing! He tears it out with one sharp tug and crushes it between his fingers like wet bread.

Mónika's fingers were still struggling with the unusual logic of the knot of Károly's tie. She was deeply disappointed by Albert. But when they reached the hospital, Albert's muscle memory came alive again. He shoved Károly up onto a hospital bed and pushed him into the corridor by the back entrance because out in the front was a queue of the eight howling victims of a fresh accident. He gave out orders . . . These sequences are familiar to everyone, they're the same as in the movies, at most the walls are more worn, the faces and coats more ragged. Commotion and confusion aplenty. By the time they reached the theatre, Károly was lying naked on the table. They had to wait for the ECG nurse who was away somewhere. She's forever going off, commented Albert with surprising patience. He mechanically turned Károly's head to one side, absently leaving his palm on Károly's cheek. He looked around for the nurse, while explaining to Mónika, the ECG nurse is a snacker, she's constantly eating, twenty years ago she was already as big as a house, her breasts spilling over the patients, but they soon felt better, a face like a frying pan, but still a sight for sore eyes . . . Mónika listened, nodding, a little dejected because her breasts weren't so big, and she'd got awfully thin in the face over the last years.

The edge of Albert's palm was brushed by a trembling eyebrow. Károly opened his eyes, screwed up his face and closed them again. He began to silently whimper.

Albert had never heard such sounds, he searched the body curiously to see where they were coming from. The sight of the naked body struck him in the face, no, not the sight but a wave of scolding air, and not the face but the chest. Károly seemed to be breathing again, not with his lungs but with his whole body—it filled with blood and, like a simmering oil stove, breathed into the room, expanding his withered aura, recovering the radiant orb, which, though it can't be seen, can be felt by some. Albert couldn't feel it. It was as though he was being tickled but couldn't say where. There was a kind of mysterious, tingling urge in the scolding wave. In any case the foot odour was washed away. Despite being an experienced diagnostician, he was stuck: In which column was he to write his sentiments? It was clear to him of course that if homoeopathic treatment was administered appropriately, the patient would respond immediately and gain a new existence at an almost dramatic rate, no sooner than sucking the medicine, a pair of soft, bright wings would grow from his body, and he would nimbly flee this cauldron of pain. Such patients look around with a cheerful smile . . . Albert laughed at the world. With a flirtatious, childish ease he gave Károly's nose a flick. Károly opened his eyes. As they tried to focus within the brilliance of the other's gaze, for some inexplicable reason, suddenly his irises cleared. Once a dark greenish grey, they were now an almost dazzling grass green. Not a cold green, but a vivid, blazing green. Filled with the fragrance of sun-licked fields. Albert almost skipped around the room, and patted Károly's face. Maybe he meant to flick Károly's nose again, but as his hand neared, he gave the red face a docile pat. And once again he reached for the nose, and again it became a pat on the cheek. He felt ashamed of his unusual behaviour. He looked up and down the bare body on public display, surveying the wrinkles, the bunions on the toes, the veins and yes, that ridiculous whatsit lurking in the grey, straggling tuft, that ridiculous little prick, yes indeed, a source of endless amusement. Yes, any moment now he'll roar with laughter. He gave Károly's cheek another pat. He paused at the eyes, then glided downwards again. And he saw something that made him shudder: Károly had an erection. He shuddered, but it wasn't the old shudder of repulsion returning. It was something completely different. He was greeted by a feeling which hadn't existed, until then.

Translated by Owen Good

LIKE A SHAGGY INK-CAP MUSHROOM

The Inspector Leaps into Action

The upturned hourglass, Christ, what an idea! They're trying to do me in! Let them! It's just they mean well. They think they run the world.

The Inspector grumbled in front of his dirty office window. Up in the sky hung grey clouds, down below dark puddles lapped up the weary light. The grass was barely awake in the narrow flower beds.

Well, I'll show them, he thrust an arm into the air, accidentally punching a passing fly, which fell dead between the radiator grill.

The Boys glanced up, silenced by their involuntary acknowledgement. But the silence he so longed for merely lasted a split second, and the usual din of the Bureau blared forth again. The telephones started ringing, the typewriters went into full swing, the pens scraped along the rough paper, cigarettes flared up, jokes cracked, and the office's however-many employees bustled about. The File Desk Girls took rasping bites from their apples and the Boys on duty questioned informers, shouted, laughed, argued, barked orders, swapped stories, and thought of everything to stop the Inspector constantly locked in the corners of their eyes from getting a modicum of peace.

I'll take no notice! Anyone who dares disobey best wear a bulletproof vest. Or know the terrain inside out. Or steer clear of the firing range.

But that's just it! The Inspector didn't even know where he ought to be. He's behind, he's lost in the fast-moving world. Which he had to keep secret but he didn't like secrets, because secrets were snake eggs in a swallow's nest, they were the threats of a world that was rotten to the core and in denial. It's good to have a death wish!

The Inspector sat at his desk. He pulled out a single strand of his grey hair, pulled it between the tips of his fingers and straightened it out. He thought—and for days now this had been his one serious plan—he'd try to stand it up on the table like a pencil. If it worked, everything would take a turn for the better.

It turned out one attempt was enough: the strand of hair stood, perfectly balanced, tall and heroic on the knotty tabletop.

Time for action then! the Inspector shouted, and circumnavigating the dumbfounded bunch, he blocked the entrance with his chair. There'll be no more scampering about here; dilly-dallying and the like. Enough mooching! I'll have silence!

The Boys watched in shock as the enormous body went into action. They didn't know this anatomy's history, they could only guess but had given up on such mental exertion a long time ago. This body attracted and repelled other bodies like a magnet. Elbowing forward and holding back. Triumphing and grovelling. Producing fluids itself and squeezing fluids out of others. Swaggering and skulking. Finding harmony and losing consciousness. Quite corpuscular, said one of the Boys cleverly. Corpulent, corrected another although he didn't know the actual meaning either.

The years had carved two parallel grooves in the undersides of the Inspector's lower thighs, which he positioned to the chair's edges and they slotted into place. He was immovable . . . He closed his eyes and, with barely any effort, freed himself completely from the shackles of time. Like massive trees, he held the loose riverbanks together, and he raised a dam on which time banked up, blocking the flow of the current so the surge of the world came to a stop. He knew no one would dare to move him from his seat because these foppish softies could guess the unleashed deluge would wash away the culpable without a trace.

Victory, victory, whispered the breeze filtering through the treetop. The Bureau had never been so silent. The whole office was frozen in ecstatic, perplexed silence. Then a deafening crash as the strand of hair toppled on the table top.

The Loudmouth Woman

Then I'll report you too! shouted the Loudmouth Woman in the door. She'd been torturing the Inspector for weeks.

No one knew what she actually wanted. The Inspector had sent his men to check her out. They were to examine everything thoroughly and weren't to come back until their briefcases were full of hard evidence. For two days he didn't see the Loudmouth or the Boys. But the Woman soon made friends with the Boys. She offered them cakes and coffee. She gave them a key. And as they were powdering the doorknobs, the glasses, the drawer handles and the flat's myriad trinkets for the umpteenth time, she was back in the Bureau nagging all day long.

On one such morning, the Inspector sprung out of his chair with an unusual impetuosity, flung open his door, tore the aluminium plaque off it and shouted at the Loudmouth Woman: Then let's just nail your name to the door, sweetheart!

The Loudmouth Woman froze and went pale. Words stuck in her throat, blocking the way for the others too. Maybe never to speak again. To suffocate even. But a second later she seemed to explode. After a brief thirty-minute spell of thunderous rage, she began to be intelligible, and five hours later her volume returned to normal. You coward. You moron. Incapable of doing your job. I'm ashamed to say where you belong, but I'll make sure your bosses recognize what's going on here, or rather, what's not. The place is dead. It's a swamp. A bog. And you're enjoying it. But you'll not be enjoying it for long! She turned and resolutely made for the door, stopped in the doorway, and threatened the Inspector again. And just before slamming the door, now bereft of its plaque, she screeched: And don't call me sweetheart, hear me? I hate that word!

The Inspector hoped that'd be the end of it. Or that he could breathe freely again after so many weeks. But nothing changed. Moreover, besides the Loudmouth Woman's constant squabbling he had to endure Internal Operations harassing him with stupid questions or silent—but all the more ominous—scrutiny on account of the Róza Mikola case.

So matters stood when one morning the very grim Inspector looked out of the window and his gaze fell upon the graveyard. He can only have seen a few gravestones, but which was a miracle considering the cemetery lay in the opposite direction, on the far side of the Bureau, on the hillside. The Inspector's office looked onto the School for the Blind, in one of whose cracked windows there was now a reflection of the cemetery grounds. This could only be the divine work of Providence, thought the Inspector, who, like everything else, didn't believe in Providence.

He stood up, walked to the window, and pulled his fingers until he'd cracked each one three times. While executing the thirty cracks he bemusedly ruminated over death. The next stop on the elevating journey towards agonizing death! Early in the morning, before the Bureau filled with people, the Inspector disappeared to take care of a few things.

When he came back, and the Boys, the Typist Girls and the File Desk Girls, the overworked Beat Cops and even the Loudmouth Woman had turned up, he walked past them like they weren't even there, almost floating through the air like a lone, ownerless balloon. When anyone asked him something, he just shrugged and smiled in silence. The Loudmouth Woman lost confidence. She struggled on pathetically, ran out of steam, and finally gave up. Now the Inspector could have done whatever he liked with her, but as the saying goes he was miles away, even though his daydreaming had taken him somewhere quite close in space and time.

He was considering going there again during lunch, but believing the workers hadn't finished, he exercised some patience and stayed. He didn't want to sour this blissful moment with a single crumb of disappointment.

Finally, all that was left was to postpone the Daily Meeting as usual. The Boys hated the Meeting, but every day they officiously asked where and when it would be to annoy their boss while plainly displaying their Schadenfreude.

No Meeting today, the Inspector said without giving a reason, donning his hat, and reaching for the door handle. He turned onto the corridor and trotted down the stairs. As he crossed the street, he recalled the day's remarkable events and as usual a sliver of doubt settled in his heart. He quickened his pace. He believed everything would become clear when he got there.

He entered the graveyard and carefully closed the squeaking iron gate behind him. He trudged up the steps and followed a narrow path. And there he was. He couldn't complain; a patch of land surrounded by thick, tall bushes with five graves in a state of neglect, proof of the tranquillity and safety there. He wanted to sit on the bench but he stood, noticing the smell of wet paint just in time. He leant over the earth-scented grave, his head slightly tipped to one side so he could make out the golden letters. He felt a shiver as he read his name.

A sense of ease came over him as if he actually had been buried and was lying in the grave. His worries melted away for although the moment had genuinely come out of the blue, he knew what to do. The splendid treasure chambers of agony had opened before him. He planned that from then on, he'd pop over more often. And at the thought of bringing a candle after dark, the sheer joy gave him goosebumps.

He stood deeply moved in front of his own grave. He became aware that there was a great deal of cats in the grave-yard, basking in the sun or hunting. There must be mice and no end of insects. He was amazed he wasn't bothered and didn't find this community irksome, because normally he couldn't bear to share his solitude with a fly.

He wanted to sit because his feet were starting to ache. He cursed the person who painted the bench. If it can't be sat on, it's not a bench. Why should he then be obligated to pay for the work? There's no point in denying it, people are incredibly irresponsible.

That's when out of the corner of his eye he caught sight of the Loudmouth Woman, climbing the main road. The Inspector was so surprised, he started madly cracking his fingers. The Woman threw a scared glance over her shoulder and picked up her pace. The Inspector almost sprinted after her.

He caught up with her under an ugly wire arbour of roses, almost running into her arms. Both jumped. Your husband? asked the Inspector, without a hello. Yes, nodded the Woman, I've been coming here every day for two years, she added with a deep sigh. I've only just started, said the Inspector, but . . . and didn't go on. He put up such a fight, she continued, he didn't want to die, he fought for two whole months, and me, I didn't get a moment's rest, it was night and day.

The Inspector sat down beside her on the iron bench. He stretched out his legs and let out a sigh. The happy excitement of the day poured from him. Fought, did you say? Did I hear you right? Surely, he thought to himself, I've got into plenty of pickles because of women, but I could never have escaped the worst of them without a woman. Tell me more about those nights and days, tell me how he fought, sweetheart!

The Inspector Meets the Pathologist

He donned his hat and galloped off like a horse. Like a camel. A camel with the Bureau's monkey on his back. How would he ever put an end to all the please-sirs? Please, sir, would you let me off a little earlier, sir? Please, sir, you don't mind, do you, sir? Please, sir, it's very important, sir!

What was her name again? Etelka? He had to escape.

The flower seller had opened on the street corner and was selling bunches of snow drops on a tin table. He'd gladly buy one but for whom? Himself?

Etelka Varga? She was forever blushing. Three times when she asked to be excused, her face changed colour like a sunlit street under passing clouds. Even her neck went red. One day he'll ask her to show her breasts too. Or maybe she thinks his Inspector's eye sees them through her clothes? Is that why she blushes?

He put the bunch of flowers tied with string in a glass, gave them some water and put them in the pantry; he'd seen his wife do that. The clink of the glass reminded him to phone her, it'd make her happy. He hoped she wouldn't arrive today. Although then he could give her the snowdrops.

He even turned the heating down. It got overly cold and he didn't sleep well. He dreamt that he's following someone along Forget-Me-Not Street, he starts stumbling; he looks down to see his trousers are around his ankles, he bends down begrudgingly, pulls them up, and they stretch so much he's almost lost in them, like in some sort of gigantic shopping bag. He woke up with the duvet wrapped around his head. It was barely past midnight. He got up, staggered out to the kitchen in his battered old slippers and opened the pantry door. When he switched on the light he found a huge cockroach on the floor, not far from the glass, and stepped on it. He deduced from its presence that his wife had been gone for six weeks now, which was how long the pesticide lasted.

He planned to hand Etelka the flowers personally but couldn't. One: Because it was as though the Boys were expecting him to, they were all in on it, and when he walked in, their gazes fell straight on the bouquet in his hand. Two: Nor could he call Etelka into his Office because it'd cause an even greater commotion than if he'd presented her with them in the open. For years he'd played with the idea of having the lot of them transferred and not hiring anyone for as long as possible.

He paced between the Boys aimlessly. Posing pointless questions, ignoring the answers and moving on. Meanwhile eavesdropping on the File Desk Girls' conversations. The spunky Beat Cops were always sniffing around there. It had to be said Beat Cops did tell the most exciting stories. They'd jump onto the chairs or under the desks as they performed the chase scenes. One of them wore a cap all summer and willingly showed everyone why: his right earlobe had been shot off. Oh, the hands of the File Desk Girls leapt to their mouths.

The Inspector had only been shot at on one occasion. Or more precisely his partner was shot at, who was always trigger-happy. That cocky dickswinger. He collected a lock of hair from every woman. His pockets were full of hair.

The Inspector had collected nothing. This struck him, as from the window he saw students on the street charging along with handcarts heaped with scrap iron. They set about prising off the manhole cover without an ounce of hesitation until the officer on duty in front of the Bureau snapped at them. As a matter of fact, at times he felt his suffering was too dreary. He closed his eyelids, tipped his head back, and imagined jumping over his wounded partner and taking off after the shooter. And then he'd get shot and clutch his chest. He pictured his current body, a 19-stone body, staggering, swaying back and forth, then slowly turning in circles, as though he were waltzing with an invisible partner. He shook his head. He didn't like thinking about his body. The Boys, ah yes, they start their days in the swimming pool, they eat vegetarian. It would've been good if his body evaporated off like a patch of snow. Leaving his soul to sob over the damp stain. If he closed his eyes he could see it all clearly and could see his soul wouldn't sob, so much as flutter with joy, because the departing body would give way for a long-sought future. How poetic . . . He could acquire a single late, but all the more passionate, love. At his age? He was going to die. That's what he was saving energy for. The Elevating! The Initiating! The Giving! The All-Knowing! For him it wasn't Love; it was Death.

He was surprised when his partner called. He didn't recognize his voice. Hence, maybe, he was filled with the cool, soft promise of the hope for happiness. The tranquillity of promise. A deep and hoarse voice. Slowly pronounced sounds. Containing an impossible amount of pain. He shuddered. Furthermore the ring of the phone had electrified him. He jumped up and almost fell on the handset. The voice's lumpy sadness. A fine, floury lumpy sadness. Immediately he thought of Death. Death was calling. Or he was about to hear news of someone else's death. He wouldn't be surprised if it was his own. There could be no greater gift. Inspector, sir, I have to relay some sad news. You've passed away, sir . . .

I'm glad I found you, said the voice. Do you know who it is?

Ádám Bokor, his old partner. Partners were rarely transferred, they were together for almost five years straight.

My wife has left me, said Bokor, and his voice faltered. I called you, I hope you don't mind. I want to ask you a favour. She's fallen in love with a younger man. There are twenty years between us, maybe that was the issue. I could have locked her down with a child, but . . . I'll get a grip, I won't cry.

He cried.

The Inspector had never heard crying like it. Perhaps he was so shaken because he couldn't see the man crying, all that came across was the nakedness. The hot, fat tears. An untouched, pure matter bursting forth from the earthy depths. Primordial matter. Hence it reminded him of Death. Suffering can be so sweet because it's experienced by the shell-less self, in the deep.

He listened to his old partner with envy. What a repulsive, superficial man he had been. He only ever dampened his thirst with beer, the Inspector had always had to wait as his partner popped into some dive. He'd sit idly in the car for hours in the afternoon sunshine and the petrol fumes, drifting hairs gathering in his nose and mouth. He found the whole thing unfair.

What happened, he meant to say but asked: When did it happen?

Three weeks ago, blubbered Bokor. Since then I just sit and wait for night to come. After it gets light I start waiting again. With her beside me I was a god. If you knew! If only I could die . . .

What's the favour? The Inspector interrupted, like he found Bokor incapable and unworthy of true death.

Call on her, she's moved, 27 Forget-Me-Not Street. Yes, Forget-Me-Not. I'm not crying. Tell her to take care of herself. Don't say anything, just see if she's all right. If she's eating okay. She was always anaemic. But only call on Tuesday after-noon. She'll be home alone. I brought her things around on Tuesday.

All weekend he couldn't stop thinking about the conver-sation. He went over it again and again. This Bokor has some time of it! He could feel the man's astounding pain down the telephone line. It came right through into the receiver, into the speaker's carbon granules. From the touch of the receiver he felt the agony of the distant voice, and like a lightning bolt, a dark-purple shadow shot from his hand to his heart. No, he'd never fantasized about having a heart attack. But he would have happily watched if the back of his hand were to slowly and subtly cover over with liver spots. He would have patiently waited as death's fluid, yes, the thick enzyme of death, slowly seeped in and flooded his body. Tuesdays are good, Tuesday's his day. He was born on a Tuesday, he became a police officer on a Tuesday, he got married on a Tuesday. It was his saddest day.

It seemed like the day would never end, no matter how much he paced about between the desks. He considered visiting the Chief Inspector, but the consequences of such a visit were unforeseeable. Often it was hours until he could leave. Or he would come out so troubled he could have crumpled himself up and tossed himself in the rubbish for the day. Etelka didn't even rise to go to the toilet, when he could have secretly called to her in the corridor, and into his Office, where she'd find something on the desk for her. Because that was his plan. He'd send her in for the bouquet. Then at most the Boys would see Etelka stealing the flowers from him. They would think all sorts about the poor girl. Oh well. As long as she didn't start making a show of her gratitude. Please, Mr Inspector, sir, may I kiss the Inspector on the cheek, sir?

Enough of these pleases and sirs! he yelled, surprising even himself. And now he too was blushing. But nobody else noticed because the moment the blood began rushing under his skin, he was halfway through the office door, slamming it behind him with due force. There was silence in the Bureau for a moment. Even the street fell deathly silent. Such a fleeting, accidental moment of deathly silence livened him up for hours. No, of course, silence has nothing to do with Death. There's no death in Silence.

He could smell Death. The flowers lay on the desk in a dark puddle like a shaggy ink-cap mushroom. The fluid of Death. He dipped his fingers in it religiously. The essence of Death, the enzyme, the power residing in every living being, and nonliving too. The matter of invisible power. An informer to those with a death wish seeking out the components of the universe. He smelled his fingers and, like he'd just sobered up,

55

became sure he had an internal eye, hidden deep within him, with which he could see Death. He could see Death at any time. There was Death now, in front of him. So clearly he didn't have to close his external eyes. The picture was so sharp he could draw it. But his drawing abilities were limited. And why would he? He didn't want to show anyone. This was his. His own death. But not just. Death is universal.

Yet before he could immerse himself in unpicking the final conclusion's endless tangles—of which naturally he would have made newer knots, being already stumped as to which death took a capital letter and which didn't—outside, one of the cretins started to howl, why won't Mr Dúró, the kit officer, understand he needs the 'dick vest', he's not losing his balls if someone slacks off. And by the time the Inspector took his earplugs from the drawer and managed to position them suitably in his ears, the philosophy of the deathly thoughts had completely dried up. Only anger remained and the uncomfortable pressure of the plugs.

He grabbed the wilted flowers in one hand and chucked them in the paper bin. Then he scooped them out, wrapped them in a used newspaper, and threw them back in again. But these Boys were quite capable of hoking through bins.

The Boys of course didn't just rifle through the bins. The Boys knew precisely how many broken pens, unopened letters, and unfinished reports lay in the Inspector's drawers. How many were left unfinished after the first or second word . . . How many broken paper clips and expired planners. Without a beat they'd tell him his shoe size and how many pairs of socks he owned, how many grey and how many black. How many of the grey pairs that slipped down his ankles and how many tighter pairs. They knew how many dirty handkerchiefs were crumpled in the pocket of his coat. Where he hid those glasses he was supposed to have worn for the last two years. How many new holes he allowed in his belt every year. Which of his legs had varicose veins. The Boys knew about each other as well, who had piles, who had a hernia, who had something else, who had how much debt, or with which kind of dirty joke they regaled the waitresses. They knew where the File Desk Girls hid their chocolates. With whom they chatted all day long on the telephone. They knew very well that Etelka Varga didn't have one Christian name but five, and one of which, Eleonóra, she hated, and dreaded the day someone would call her by it. Moreover, they knew that every night she exercised her breasts and that she had nicknamed one Pinky, its counterpart Perky.

Leaving without raising suspicion was no easy task. He did his best to reproduce his Monday departure; going through the same motions, donning his hat, tossing his coat over his shoulder and stopping in front of the File Desk Girls. But Etelka hadn't asked to be excused earlier as she usually did, she was still in her chair. This threw him off. To make matters worse, she asked him: Are you leaving already Inspector? What can I say to that, he grumbled, and wheezing, hurried out the door.

Grey, snow-scented clouds covered the town. The morning spring had vanished without a trace. He didn't care. At most he was sorry he'd missed the transition. Due to the town's geographic situation, the fronts coming in from the distant sea arrived around noon, during work, hindering him from witnessing in contemplation the stirring, preterhuman sadness of change.

Upon pressing the bell, a window curtain fluttered across the yard but nobody appeared. He rang a second time, and a third. Eventually the wife appeared. The tall girl was so terribly young and fragile that he asked if he had the right address. The girl, the wife, that is, looked at him with suspicion. When their eyes met she immediately looked away.

Do you have a minute? Ádám sent me.

Tears filled her eyes. She stepped inside without a word. The Inspector watched the rolling hips. But she herself looked stiff as two boards. Strained. Maybe she knows what I'm thinking.

He asked me to call in.

We agreed he wouldn't send any messages.

He hasn't. He'd just like to know if you're well.

I am.

Are you eating properly? He said you're anaemic.

It's hard for me too. Honestly. But at least I've lost the lump in my throat.

It was oddly hot in the room. Perhaps it was the ceramic stove. It was too well stocked. But she was wearing a thick jumper. A drop of condensation ran down the window, he saw it through the nylon curtain. It wasn't the heat which was strange, it was the stench. The stench of heat. He removed his hat and felt his forehead glisten.

You're very young, if you don't mind me saying.

I was still in school when we met.

She pointed to the armchair. The Inspector unbuttoned his coat and as he moved towards the chair his eyes circled the room. Not a full circle, but a sector of a few degrees at most. He couldn't bear to take his eyes off her. Bit by bit he could feel himself getting involved with something still far in the distance. Ceremoniously, falteringly, he readied himself to speak—he drew out the time. Like an unexpected guest hoping to be offered a glass of something. Her face began to fill with a peculiar beauty. The two pin-sized nooks in the outer corners of her eyes welled with a terrible sadness.

Tell him one or two months, and you'll see how you feel.

I don't want to go back.

Then tell him you've had enough. Any man would be better than him, hit him with that.

What do you want from me?

He asked me to call on you. This isn't easy for me either. Sorry.

Warmth suddenly flooded the Inspector's stomach. He could feel he was about to blush. He too was sensitive to words. Often one was enough to ruin a life. Incidentally his life had been ruined by old Guszti Ridegh, an internally exiled count who lived in the yard, who once said . . . It doesn't bear repeating! He bent over and fixed his socks. That day he was wearing slack grey ones. He pulled them up his ankles.

It wouldn't hurt to wear elastic tights for your varicose veins, she said.

Now he really blushed.

Are you not too warm?

I like the purr of the stove.

Certainly noisy.

It's like there's someone in the room.

Are you alone a lot?

Yes.

Is the other man in the police?

There is no other man.

Ádám reckons some new love . . .

I don't want to hear that word. Ádám is the vilest person on the planet. All I've wanted for a while now is to die.

The Inspector leapt up with a gleeful heart. I have to go, he stammered. Then fumbled for a while with his buttons, he kept getting them wrong. Coincidence? Yes, another coincidence. Correct. Every sign suggests that there exists some sort of plan. That there's a kind of matter inside people that drives them together. In their dreams. In their thoughts. In their bodies. Of course, the stench! He let out a sigh. From another point of view, there are no coincidences. And Death never comes by coincidence. He breathed his lungs full. Very nearly knocking over a pile of books on the table.

Are you studying?

I'm a doctor.

Medical books?

I'm preparing to specialize.

An internist?

A pathologist.

A pathologist?

It was Ádám's idea.

And do you like it?

It's interesting.

Do you study a lot?

I do.

And the death enzyme? Ever heard of that?

The Inspector Gives the Fig Sign

The Inspector liked jokes about policemen. He wasn't a joke teller himself, but it made him happy whenever he came across a new one. A squad of policemen and a squad of firemen get on a double-decker bus. The police have been upstairs taking in the city's sights for a while when the fire captain comes up to say hello. He sees them, white in the face, holding onto their seats for dear life. What's all this, he asks. It's all right for you, says the chief, you've got a driver. He agreed with whoever conceived the joke: all police are idiots. And the most idiotic among them was Norbi Szécsényi. A calamity! He would creep over to the Inspector's desk, coming so close his bottom button tapped against the tabletop and when the Inspector asked what he wanted, he stretched out an arm and regarded his watch: mee-ting-time! When he pursed his lips, his top lip touched his nose; what a pillock! Maybe you think you're a sniffer dog, son!

All morning the Inspector had been shivering. It wasn't that the flu had got the better of him, not this time. He was shuddering at the sound of Norbi's name. Norbi! Norbika! Nooorbertooo! Three days ago he got his freshly whitewashed office back, but the thin walls amplified the faintest noise like an acoustic instrument. Shutting himself in was pointless, he

61

couldn't pursue his suffering like this, and if he couldn't suffer, he lamented over the past. That fatal moment when he'd been made inspector preyed on his soul. Even then he was quite past his prime.

He kicked the chair out from behind him, tore open his door and shouted: Norbi!

He'd been too hasty. Norbi was nowhere to be seen, of course, nevertheless the rest enthusiastically joined in, calling his name. And boy did they! It was as if they were yelling: Inspector Dolt! Because the reason he couldn't find Norbi was not that he was nowhere to be found, Norbi was there, but his eyes weren't sharp enough to see him, nor his ears sensitive enough to hear him, he was too slow to spot him. You're out of your depth! So shouted the insolent Boys and yet more insolent File Desk Girls.

Primarily due to its reliability, the Inspector liked thinking of Death with a capital D. There had never been a case of it not coming. At times it descended on people like a guillotine, at times it stole into the room inch by inch, creeping up the wall to the window like damp, or night-scented stock. He would have happily married Death. None could be less reliable than women, including his own wife, though she always wore the same type of hat. He often got the feeling that Norbi Szécsényi was a woman. Not only because of his silky skin and freckles, but because of how elusive he was. And of course it's worth mentioning the world of arithmetic and logical operations. Because when the Inspector tried, he could still manage integral calculus. He could explain how a television worked, a telephone, a four-stroke engine. Norbi on the other hand knew nothing, and yet he shimmered like a bird of paradise.

It never occurred to Norbi that he might know nothing. Anything he didn't know was bollocks. He would have said integral calculus was a crutch for small-mindedness. It's the person asking the question one has to see. If the Inspector ever asked him whether he'd told the Boys that the Meeting was cancelled, he replied that the Boys knew everything. At which the Inspector nervously scratched his head. His scalp itched whenever he had a problem. He privately contemplated Norbi's soft profile; his long hair, his doughy double chin, his fashionable small-lensed silver glasses. And he saw the scale of the bubble surrounding him. But Norbi was much, much smaller than this bubble, positively puny. His lanky figure didn't fill the chair, but his bubble filled the entire Bureau, it reached beyond the walls of the whole building. Not so much a bubble, as risen dough, that was Norbi. And unquestionably a dough leavened with hypocrisy.

There wasn't a soul in the Bureau who didn't complain. The Detective Chief Inspector about the ministry, the Boys about each other (and privately about the Inspector), the File Desk Girls about nail polish, the nail polish about competing products, competition about life. Yes, the incessant, never-ending lamentations were a part of life. But Norbi never complained about anything or anyone. Yes, he badmouthed everyone, but that's a different kettle of fish. He was a content man, people must have thought. And consequently, that it was worth following in his footsteps, or living as he did.

As far as Norbi's footsteps were concerned, the Inspector was sure they lead to the Public Prosecutor's office. If he wasn't grassing, who was?

The Inspector, however, had made another mistake, but again not a big one. Norbi had never been near the Public Prosecutor's, but he did frequent the Canteen, which had two exits: one for the Bureau, the other for the Prosecutor's Office. (According to the exact topography there was a third exit that opened past the warehouse onto a narrow alleyway where an iron door led to the Prison. Supposedly the hinges were never greased because the rust never set in.) Norbi spilled the beans on this and that in the Canteen, as if he was chatting to his morning milky coffee. Either he said hello to the canteen girl Aranka, or he threw a cheerful smile to Imre, the Newsvendor: so, auld Imre, I can come fishing with you today, there's no Meeting. And his voice carried beyond the Canteen, and transformed along the corridors of the Prosecutor's Office into a confidential report, and as such slipped into the Prosecutor's ears. All sorts of things were learnt via those winding, fur-lined passages. Such confidential reports of course were dashed by a grain of logic, or a pinch of scruple, but the Prosecutor also possessed a pinch of pure malice, and so the poor Inspector was constantly formulating Counter-Reports, quite enough to disturb his peaceful suffering. And a restless suffering was good for diddly-squat. How could he write a Counter-Report to a Report that didn't exist?

Norbi's rambling words manifested inside the Prosecutor. Or to put it differently, Norbi's invisible actions became decipherable in the Prosecutor's ordinances, just as forces operating in our subconscious are revealed in our dreams, or a phrase accidentally let slip. Moreover, one could say he was the biting end of the Prosecutor's cracking whip. The Inspector looked up at Norbi and saw the grinning maw of the Prosecutor.

On the Inspector's table there stood a nickel-plated, spinning ashtray which sucked the ash in at the touch of a button. More precisely, the button was nickel and that's where the Inspector saw his reflection. At that moment the minute caricature flashing on the nickelled button, an apelike shrivelled skull and bulging nose, seemed accurate.

He wished he was ash and lived in an urn. He had a new idea to buy a coffin, bring it into his office and periodically lie in it. The problem was he now had enough experience of suffering to know that the implementation of any plan would result in complete failure. Firstly, a bespoke coffin wouldn't even fit. And cremation had its stipulations too.

When the madness had reached its apex, coinciding with noon, he resorted to something reserved for the rarest of cases: he visited the Detective Chief Inspector. Often it was enough to merely step through the padded door and at once the ringing of telephones, the clacking of typewriters and the constant shrieking vanished. The Detective Chief Inspector offered him a seat, while theatrically tidying the papers laid out in front of him. Then he started into the usual lamentations, his duties, which he'd no time for because he only has one head and two hands, and what's more, his friends in the ministry had forgotten about him.

The Detective Chief Inspector had difficulty rolling out the words because he started his day with a brandy. A few actually, and the fourth straight from the bottle. The Inspector watched tensely but soon lost the thread and began to be restless, his scalp itchy, his nose blocked, and on top of that, he glimpsed a shadow dart across the room like a bat. Among the words he couldn't locate the subject, or the predicate, or the object, and within moments the syntactical disarray had exhausted him. If he turned his attention elsewhere he got lost again in the din drifting through the walls like a spirit from the nether world, but not a reassuring one. Slowly, however, he returned at least to the level where he could seek refuge. And then went one higher: he grew sleepy.

So anyway, anyway, the reiterated words flushed him from the thicket, words which, plopped more manageably into the net of his sobered awareness, anyway, we need to take the bull by the horns. Yes, the Prosecutor's sick, bloody sick, but they can't postpone the visit again, he's going to beg the Prosecutor for forgiveness, and he suggests the Inspector follow his example.

Tomorrow's no good, said the Inspector, searching for a way out, there's the Szabó Gang hearing. He was out of it, he hoped, yet the Detective Chief Inspector, excelling himself, took a tough decision: Let's go now then. Come on!

The sides of the wet road were heaped with dirty snowdrifts. The two men had to tramp halfway up Sirály Hill. They had gone by car but then walked because they couldn't pull into the driveway. He's going to die, they've stopped clearing the snow. They plodded through the slush. I'm going to catch a cold, muttered the Detective Chief Inspector hopefully. When he got a cold, his voice crooned more mellowly, and his mellow voice made even the Secretary's ears turn red.

'Is the Prosecutor home?' asked the Boss in a rasping voice from the boy standing in the doorway, who had a haircut exactly like Norbi Szécsényi's. The boy nodded with a grin as he fixed the lock with a screwdriver. Perhaps he's changing the lock?

They climbed stairs, crossed dark rooms and soon arrived at a dimly lit, frighteningly spacious room with a flickering gas fireplace. The Inspector was hit by the sweet smell of death. He breathed it in deep to stow away as much as possible, so later he could regurgitate it in more peaceful circumstances. The haughty Prosecutor lay like a tiny mound of rags on top of the incomprehensibly large bed. He looked like a rain-drenched molehill. He grunted as he sat up on his elbows, glanced at his visitors, and weakly lay down again. They thought that would be all, but it wasn't. He opened his eyes again. He had difficulty breathing. The Inspector's teeth started chattering again. He wasn't a man of words, maybe that's why he had such difficulty writing Reports. But who could put into words what he experienced there?

At most what he saw. He saw a chewed-up and matted little animal that had patched its maw with shreds of the Prosecutor's face. Where its eyes should have been gaped dark cavities so large there was barely any space between for its pointed snout.

The Detective Chief Inspector had also gone quiet. He began sweating so profusely that his underwear soaked through, then the seat of his trousers, then later in the car his coat too, inspiring staff members to guess at the cause. Neither felt they could resolve the situation, even if they stayed all day. Both belonged to that age group that turns on the TV and sits in front of it, regardless of the programme, until the screen became fuzzy grains.

The Prosecutor raised his head. Most probably trying to recover his unquestionable superiority, when his head fell back on the pillow. He now noticed that his condition too could win him considerable superiority, and then some. He let himself be taken by the tumultuous death throes, and let out such a rattle both officers turned to feeble house mice.

Without a touch of hyperbole, we might say the usually disdainful Prosecutor was grateful to his visitors. He was suddenly at ease. First, during his demise, he thought he would soon be better off. He would be fine, these two unlucky fellows, however, would have to wait their turn. He made peace with his condition since he would soon leave it all behind. Nor would there ever be another alarm clock. He felt real catharsis. He wanted to beckon them closer but hadn't the strength, barely managing to straighten his arm at the elbow. His hand dropped to the edge of the bed, seemingly clutching something intended for his visitors.

The Boss prodded the Inspector. Perhaps he meant to give them the stamped approval of their absolution, or perhaps the informer's report. The Inspector hadn't been prodded like that since he worked a beat; he stepped forward automatically, bewildered. He took three paces and leant closer to see inside the half-open fist. But of course, he found nothing, except: the Prosecutor's thumb thrust obscenely between his index and middle fingers. It was a puny, shrivelled fig sign.

He quietly returned to his position. What is it? the Detective Chief Inspector looked at him, raising his eyebrows. Nothing, he answered, shaking his head. Then maybe let's go, said his boss, as if they'd got what they came for. Let's, nodded the Inspector, digging his hands in his pockets. And they crept through the rooms and down the stairs, hearts beating in their throats. The Prosecutor had always been a ghastly character, and after a cheerful farewell, it wasn't uncommon for him to then holler and berate his departing visitor, flinging caustic remarks at the backs of their necks. But now he hadn't the strength even to breathe.

At the corner in front of the Bureau, the Inspector got out of the car, pleading he be dismissed since he'd be on duty that night. He still had death's fragrance in his nose and wanted to bring it home. He believed he had found what he was searching for. Or rather, had simply stumbled across it. By the time he reached home, he knew that what he'd discovered had such weight, it could crush him to death. Rushing into the hallway in his overcoat, he realized he had no business with real death, he was light years away from that. Previously he had had similar bouts of depression: feeling more or less that he was an atrocious Inspector; that the Boys were much more competent; that he ought to retire. But then he would remember Norbi, and the spite would harden him. Now, however, the basis of his entire life had been shaken. Death made no sense. He had to return to life. To buy a car, to travel the world. To have lovers. To dart from one to the other, like a bee from flower to flower. To start drinking brandy. He would read. He would write his memoirs. He would fill his time with pure nonsense because the most personal, the most precious deed in his whole life had been a failure.

He called in sick and didn't go for duty. That night he had unusually vivid thoughts of Death. Occasionally he burst into laughter. Him, him taking Death to be his wife, and living happily ever after, what a load of crap, as big as the Bureau, bigger! As big as the Prosecutor's Office, Police Station and Prison put together! Death was such an unpredictable, beguiling, inscrutable, terrifying, ghastly, real thing. The Prosecutor knew. And that fig sign was for him alone. This one's for you, boyo, this is how much you know!

He slept badly and went in early. He found Norbi Szécsényi there who had taken over from his duty. He hurried past Norbi without a word, then two minutes later called him into his office. I'm sorry, son, I'm sorry, you've no grip on reality, he explained, and thrust his thumb between his fingers. And this, he jabbed the fig sign under Norbi's nose, arrived for you from the Prosecutor. There you go, boy, that's yours. And he felt sorry for the drowsy, skew-eyed boy gawking at the fig sign. At the same time, he felt an implacable hatred: How could this hopelessly cretinous, moronic, incompetent boy possibly be the most competent among them?

Translated by Owen Good

AT THE WESTERN GATE

I should first point out that in the previous two or three years, the blows of fate—drought, earthquake, floods—had followed each other in rapid succession. At that time, my father was still an active dancer at the Opera, although it was growing ever harder for him to lift his partners. He complained continuously of the ballerinas' gluttonous habits, not for a minute thinking about his back. When on stage, of course, he ploughed through the rehearsals and performances without a word of reproach; but ever since my father commented to the director Sorbán—a vain prick—that the dancers should perhaps be hired on the basis of their talents, Sorbán had turned against him, looking for the most trifling pretext to give my father the sack. All of this was nothing, though, compared with what we were about to face.

Our house, which had been built by my father's grandfather, was located on the eastern edge of the city; it rose up like a castle, at the end of Acacia Street, to the crowns of the trees near the gently sloping bank of the river. When the refugees began to arrive, they knocked at our door first, perhaps thinking our house, with its wooden balconies and roof gables, to be a kind of sanitorium. My father generously provided them with food, even slipping some money into their hands. When others came knocking on the door in the middle of the night, he would clamber out of bed, grabbing something to eat from the refrigerator or the larder.

After that, however, there were no more beggars. It was said throughout the city that they could not make their way up the river because of the recent flooding, and that several had drowned near the Gyöngyös farmstead. Silence descended upon us. My father continued to grumble about Sorbán from dawn to dusk, and of course about the ballerinas as well. My mother would smile with maliciously enigmatic glee, although between us I could say that while my father's fidelity appeared to be untarnished, my mother might have had something to hide. Once a rag merchant moved in with us, ruddy faced and grizzled; she followed him everywhere, yet at the same time was visibly revolted . . . Perhaps it was precisely that dark, deep repugnance that captivated her, and something had happened between them, because afterwards she always shuddered if she happened to pass by the ramp leading up to the attic. For a while, I thought that something similar had come down to me from my mother's dark side, as an inheritance, but later I realized that its source was completely different.

And then, from one day to the next, the animals disappeared, even though before they had been assembling in vast numbers around the house. One evening, as it was growing dark, two foxes appeared in front of the kitchen window overlooking the garden. They circled around intensely, their movements slow and swaying. The first one darted and capered in a wide circle around the second, at times from left to right, at times in the opposite direction. The other moved in a circle around its own axis, its fox gaze riveted upon its companion. Suddenly, they noticed us: they raised their heads and looked at us for several long minutes. The next day we waited for them in vain; the dormice and the martens too had moved away. They've all taken off, my mother said, and shuddered again as if she were in front of the attic ramp. I, however, could not free myself from the fox's gaze. Wherever I looked, I saw that gaze lurking, a mute disembodied creature underneath the garden shrubbery.

Then the birds disappeared: only the crows and the jackdaws darkened the sky like seeds cast from a sack above the distant streaks of forest, near the farmstead once held by the Gyöngyös family, though of course long ago, at the beginning of collectivization, everything had been ploughed under. Perhaps they had been drawn by the raging whirlpools, seeking their nourishment among the liquid siftings cast up by the current on the shore, but the fact is that in the morning, they were already circling above, their shapes visible against the moistly glittering sky. They were so far away that you could not hear their cawing. In the city, silence reigned.

So it was all the more surprising when one morning we became aware of a sizeable group of people in front of our house, standing among the trees of the small, nameless park. There were six of them to be precise, two adults and four children—one of whom we took to be already grown up but who, it turned out later, was barely thirteen. It was enough to cast one fleeting glance at their plastic bags and muddied shoes to see that they had come from the East.

The father was dressed in black, with a white shirt and black tie. The people from the East always dressed strangely, and their speech was strange as well. Their gestures were marked by a kind of fumbling solemnity. He was a priest, we discovered when he rang at our door that evening, as dusk began to fall. It was hard for us to understand what he was saying; not because of his accent, but because he used lengthy, archaic expressions. They had done nothing all day but sit on a bench under the acacia trees and stare into space. All six on one bench. They were despondent, and the little ones did not even scamper about, which was unusual. We had always imagined that the children in the East ran around wild all day; it was said of them that they were part savage.

We spied on them from the window of the smaller front room. They sat there like people waiting for the rainfall to stop, but with no idea as to what would happen then. As darkness began to fall, the priest rang our doorbell.

Necessary to mention as well is the wooden shed at the far end of our garden, which (ever since gas had been laid on in the house) had been used for storing tools, as well as for drying plums and herbs for tea. An ancient pear tree, nearly collapsing under the weight of its countless fine-grained yellow pears, stood in front of the shed; thanks to the recent rains, the wasps had not pilfered as much of the fruit as usual. The priest, as he was sitting on the bench, stared uninterruptedly at the wooden shed, then at the luxuriant pear tree in front of it, and of course it was not hard to guess the direction of his thoughts. Who knows what the crux of the matter was: would he feel worse if he climbed up onto the fence and stuffed his pockets with fruit from the lower branches, making him a thief, or if he merely asked for the fruit, making him a beggar.

My father went once again to the front door. He returned after a short time and, nearly laughing, informed us of the priest's request. He wanted to stay in the little wooden house with his family for a few days.

As my father went out again, we feared he would do something rash. His nature was accommodating, even morbidly generous. We were afraid we'd have to eat dinner with the strangers, or else that they would settle permanently in the woodshed where we, the children, had our own comfortably furnished nook. But our father showed a new side of his character. As he sat down again at the table, he was grumbling about why they had come just now. He was alluding to the fact that the children and the elderly had been sent to camps weeks ago because of the typhus epidemic—the new arrivals were obviously pestilent with every kind of bacterium possible. I'm not going to let them dump that on us! And then, why did the priest desert his flock? My father spoke these words very gravely, although he never went to church and personally knew no priests himself. This phrase became so fixed in his mind that it reminded him again of his own work and his own responsibilities, and without being prompted, he began to list everything that was wrong at the rehearsals: how could you even rehearse when the carpets were full of holes, the parquet floors thick with bumps, the mirrors blotchy. The passion of duty, in a word, burned in my father like a flame, and he would still return to the Opera as a conscientious artist, with a sense of his calling, to make a few twists and turns at the bar. My mother, who was usually not as generous as my father, all the same took bread and some fruit to the priest and his family, and maybe some more plastic bags as well.

75

Their lodgings were actually not too uncomfortable: the rain never penetrated the thick cover of jasmine bushes. We often played there with the other children in the neighbourhood. I had long been planning to spend an entire night there as a test of my own courage.

My father arrived home late, but we were upstairs and heard what he was saying to my mother. He did not like that man; he sensed an ulterior motive. The priest had picked out this very house for himself and his family. First the woodshed, then the house . . . There had been many similar instances, my mother surely had heard of them too. No, my mother replied, she hadn't heard. Well, they talk about it, my father affirmed, and like someone alarmed by his own words, took the flashlight and went outside to check if all the doors and windows were shut. We watched the circle of light from the windows as it fluttered fearfully here and there. Then he came back and declared that it was stupid to not have listened to the children, because without a dog the entire house was at their mercy. As if our house were a giant, idiotic reptile, incapable of defending itself against attack.

No one broke into the house. The priest and his family came up with a few thick poles, stuck them into the ground behind the bench, cut up some of the plastic bags to stretch across them, and began to put their things in order. I liked their little hut, especially since the little bench was promoted to the status of a terrace, where one could sit outside without a care in the world.

My father, however, watched them with ever-greater anxiety. After lunch, he always performed his role for us, his feet stamping wildly by the finale. He would start by standing in the middle of the kitchen, torso convulsed, and in the midst of such crashing and cracking noises that we thought the roof was about to collapse onto our heads; then he would start his diatribe against everything in our town: ever-greater neglect, nothing was properly cared for, as if doomsday were around the corner—which of course many would use for their own profit. Then came the good-for-nothing Sorbán: he had engaged a new dancer again, one with no sense of rhythm, but just right for his prick. Yes—here he turned vague, taking alarm at the disapproving wrinkle in my mother's eyebrows— the director was exactly like a squirrel who would go plunging from the tree without his bushy tail. Finally, he quickly veered onto the topic of the priest and his family, and here he stumbled. Leave them alone, can't you see, they're not bothering anyone, my mother reassured him. But I told them I won't give them the shed, so they can leave already! Then Sorbán again, Sorbán who sent his own mother to the nursing home.

One Sunday morning, when no rehearsals or performances were scheduled in the Opera, my father went out to the priest and his family, and performed his role for them, from the twisting at the waist up to the howling at the end. He went so far as to grab the priest's arm and swing him around as he used to do with his female partners in his youth. The priest, however, instead of pirouetting, fell clumsily across the bench, tearing through one of the walls of their makeshift hut, and then lay stretched out on the ground. Instantly, my father calmed down, but began a loud disquisition on his moral principles to any incidental gaping bystander. If he had taken them in, it would have put the priest and his family in an unfair position—they would have become envious, or merely waiting for the bread of charity, mouths slung open. Which was, of course, the lesser of many evils, yet it was clear that no matter how much the situation would improve, they would never know, and never be willing to return home. Who knows just how far they could go in their petrified hopelessness! We've all heard of similar instances . . . If, however, he didn't let them in, the result would be that they would lure the others with their little hut, poisoning the lives of every one of us. Of course, he could see that the priest was basically a decent, upright man, but those who would come next would clearly be much more aggressive, quarrelsome, uncouth.

It is hard to know the precise cause—whether the physical or the verbal onslaught—but the next day the priest and his family began preparing to leave. They packed up all of their belongings and stared with disquiet at the birds circling low in the overcast sky, or towards the West, thought at one time to be the promised land.

But I need to leap back a few days. One afternoon, the priest's daughter and the elder of her younger brothers somehow ended up at our house, and we—the two of them, my younger sisters, and my cousin who lived nearby—played hide-and-seek until evening. It happened that at one point we hid with the girl in the cellar. We were squeezed tight against each other in the narrow space, my palm pressed against her breast. In quick response, her hand lightly touched my groin. At first I felt her gesture to be impudent; both indignant and ashamed, I avoided her until the end of the game. That night, though, after I lay down, my vagrant thoughts ceaselessly wandered around the question of what I had let slip by me.

I even found out her name, Juliska Szabó. She could have been a relative, I thought, because my mother's maiden name had been Szabó. But I didn't mention that to anyone. After my father had fallen out with the priest, and the family had begun to gather up their things, I went down to the garden and beckoned to her over the fence, so I could hurl one of the insults learnt from my father at her: I did not want to leave that moment when she touched my groin unanswered. She prowled across the damp grass as if searching for a fallen object, and then hurriedly whispered: Meet me in the wooden shed. In the meantime, I heard my mother's voice calling me to lunch. I went into the house and sat down at the table so that I could see out from the kitchen window. I watched her as she climbed across the fence near the cornel bush and ran to the wooden shack. My heart was in my throat as I rushed there too at breakneck speed.

I stepped into the gloomy herb-scented cabin, then bolted the door from the inside, even pushing a basket filled with jam jars in front of it. An orange-red light stole in through the tiny filthy window. There was a bed in the shack; she was already lying on it. She was completely naked. Paralyzed, teeth chattering, I gaped at her luminous body. Or rather, I stared with shuddering eyes. Panicking, I stammered that my father would be coming immediately. At that, she made a grab for her clothes. I saw how truly poor they were. And most ridiculously, how for all her girlhood, she was wearing boys' underwear with a slit in front. This seemingly sober observation brought me back to my senses. I wanted recompense for my teeth chattering of a moment ago. I grabbed at the bottom of her blouse and began to tug at it for her to take it off. She didn't want to any more. We began to scuffle. The musty reek of poverty on her body infuriated me, yet I wanted to slip inside her. She was scrawny but cunning, and easily slid out from under me. I jumped up and twisted her arm behind her; she was mere skin and bones, like a chicken leg. Panting heavily, we plunged down onto the groaning springs, I pressed down hard on her with my stomach. She withstood this mutely for a bit, as if thinking, then turned out from under me, wrenched the basket away from the door, tore off the lock. I leaped after her in vain but could not reach her.

Thinking it over, I must not have run after her, because before I could move, she looked around and turned to stone. As if in her eyes there was the gaze of the fox that for weeks now had been haunting me. And completely to the point, for the fox was merely the temporary owner of that gaze: in reality, it belonged to someone else. That someone was there with me in the wooden shack. It rubbed against my sides, prodded my loins repeatedly, settled down upon me: indeed, it was as if a demon that could never be expelled had taken up residence inside me for good.

Translated by Ottilie Mulzet

open Lesson

On the night of 23 August 1944, the Romanian army crossed the Carpathian Mountains. The local inhabitants welcomed them with open arms, and risking their own lives, helped eradicate enemy shooters' nests. Sporadically, fierce fighting broke out; the merciless Horthyist occupiers defended mercilessly. Wipe that smirk off your face, Lakatos! In Tölgyesi Pass, a Hungarian soldier tied himself to his machine gun and, though he bled from multiple wounds, went on gunning down Romanian soldiers in their droves. After three days he was finally snuffed out. Sixty-six serving soldiers silenced, a majestic memorial was erected by descendants in their honour, I recommend a visit. The sixty-seventh would be the killer . . . Open the window, Pongrácz, it's musty in here, I'm getting hoarse. We'll continue next lesson.

But the next lesson turned out quite differently. Your teacher, Comrade Szilágyi, has fallen ill, said Eleonóra Vízi, and I'll be filling in. What's that, boy, what seems to be the problem? What's your name?

Perhaps Comrade Szilágyi wasn't even ill, because it was the height of May, and for a while the chlorine washbasin, a sure sign of an outbreak, hadn't been seen in front of the

81

porter's hut. Perhaps Mrs Vízi just needed the school's best class to hold her open lesson. The dress rehearsal was held downstairs beside the staff room in the history lab. Mrs Vízi had had the room equipped purely for her personal use. She could, her husband was the ideological canvassing secretary on the City Party Committee.

Mrs Vízi had begun using multimedia methods before the term even existed. On the classroom wall was an enormous map, shipped straight from the Bucharest School Supplies Factory, with a hundred tiny bulbs on it, each one marking the site of a significant event. She assigned the pressing of the buttons to Miklós, who diligently listened to the lesson until a name was mentioned, at which point Eleonóra gave him a meaningful look and he pressed the appropriate button on the vast control desk. It wasn't his fault the map gave up the ghost. The city of Alba Iulia started lighting up for Brașov and Satu Mare for Giurgiu. First she called Miklós a cretin, then when she understood there was a technical issue at hand, she sent for Old Antal, the technology teacher, who was prepared to rewire it for her but hesitated it would entail several weeks of meticulous work, at which Mrs Vízi ran from her history lab in a fit of tears.

Eleonóra Vízi needed one more exam to obtain the highest teaching degree, which in turn she needed to become a school director. Something had to be done. She liked to make a show. And since she had always been proud of her multimedia methods, which she termed methodologically multifaceted, she devised the idea of involving the whole school in her open lesson, where, using her favourite word, she'd have an 'ad-hoc' company of pupils act out one of the history textbook's most elevating chapters.

The examiners arrived for an assembled history lesson, but the school inspectors also attended, plus three of the City Party Committee, and even Comrade Dulea's deputy.

'Mihai Viteazul unites the three Romanian realms of Wallachia, Moldavia, and Transylvania,' this was the title of the lesson. Since little time had remained to practise the scenes, the pupils were allowed to keep their history books in their hands and if necessary could peek to see what was next. Péter Sebe, the prize pupil, was Voivode Mihai Viteazul, 'Michael the Brave', author of a united Romania; Viktor Kovács was Pătrașcu, Mihai's son; and the third pupil in the class, Tibor Lippai, was his chief commander, Bilasku. The weaker pupils, as always, got the losing side; András Báthory who ends up impaled in the forest went to the never-listening, forever-distracted Szeredai, and Zsigmond Báthory to Miklós. The traitor Basta went to Koroknai; Ieremia, Voivode of Moldavia, went to Öcsi Haller. Emperor Rudolf II went to Tündik, and Little Tempfli performed Laszki, the Polish delegate.

The lesson began in the assembly hall, but afterwards, the short introduction continued in the schoolyard with the beautiful scene when Voivode Mihai Viteazul marches into Alba Iulia. From the supplies room, the pupils were given two colours of school kits to wear, unlike in PE class where Mr Bordás wouldn't even let them use the leather football. Meanwhile the teaching staff, inspectors, Party leaders, and the band of mildly liquor-breathed examiners poured into the first-floor corridor and watched the events below from the windows. For a while nothing happened, but then Szeredai forgot his role, that is, he failed to remember which part he was given, and since the boy thought highly of himself, stood before the victorious regiment and started issuing orders as Voivode Mihai. Sebe hissed at him to get out of the way, to which Szeredai shoved Sebe, who fell flat on his back. The school went deathly silent. Szeredai, to mitigate the embarrassment, held his book out and read Mihai's speech, in which he names himself the country's unifier and vows to be a just ruler, to gather the lords and the people both under his banner, and to protect the nation from external enemies. But this only exacerbated things, as many of his classmates still believed he was András Báthory, due to be banished and impaled.

Truth be told, among the school inspectors there were more provocatively natured colleagues who, although knowing Eleonóra's promotion was inevitable, were happy to throw a spanner in the works for the head honcho's wife, hence one inspector, recognizing the confusion, formed a megaphone with his hands and called down like a film director: Let the battle commence!

The prize pupils playing the victors were shrimps, so in the surging schoolyard below, the battle had hardly started when it was already won. The pupils playing the losers barely had to move, the yard was cleared of the appointed victors with ease, indeed, they took one look around, and already they were alone in the middle of the schoolyard.

Class IV-A, taught by Arthur Caricas, who hadn't been given parts because they were preparing for their final exams, couldn't stand by and watch the II-B kids, who crushed them a week ago in the school basketball tournament final, triumph so easily, and so with a nod from their form-master, Class

IV-A set about reoccupying the schoolyard. They had better numbers, and naturally that difference of two years counted.

Eleonóra, meanwhile, was foraging in her history lab, she always got hungry when she was nervous. She took her lunch from her lacquer handbag, unbundled the little brown casserole, lifted the blue lid, and inhaled the heavenly aromas, as blueish-brownish hues spilled across her face with the delicious grimace of anticipation. Then, reaching in two fingers, she picked out a roundish, breaded and browned morsel, popped it in her mouth, and crunched it between her sharp rows of teeth. It could have been a little boy's testicle, such was the size of that breaded and browned morsel, and by all means, when it burst, Eleonóra's powdered cheeks filled with a warm gleeful glow. And at that very moment, there came from the schoolyard the first battle cry of II-B, Miklós's class. Their army was built on the winning basketball team, on tried-and-tested positions and formations, calling numbers that represented perfected manoeuvres. And so, they took up the fight against the physically advantaged IV-A. Nor should it be overlooked, that playing for the latter was Ernő Géza Nagy, the loathed secretary of the school's Young Communist League.

For a while, Miklós was happy to charge around, in his own way, but then, as usual, he tired of it all. For weeks now, he had been waiting for something inevitable. He had been helpless, confused, and full of doubts. When he lay down at night, sleep evaded him for hours. He repositioned his bed below the window to gaze at the stars and fantasize about the infiniteness of the universe, but his thoughts wouldn't let up. He was occupied with an event much closer at hand, with its opportunities, with its consequences, but chiefly with the intricate planning of its imminent occurrence. Since becoming entangled in his plans, he would assiduously arrange them, only for them to fall apart by the morning, and force him to start over. One night, mustering all his courage, he called Juli, what's more, he confessed to her how much he liked her, the next day, however, he didn't dare look at her, during the breaks he avoided her, though Juli plainly kept apart from her friends, and stood alone in the corridor, leaning out the window. Now they had their chance because their allocated parts allowed them to wander off. More precisely, Zsigmond Báthory was entrusted by his uncle to save the treasury, to take it across the Carpathians, to Moldavia, where even birds daren't fly, and cats have five legs; of course, it was all smoke and mirrors, a simple diversion: the vengeful Székely warriors wouldn't give pursuit to Cardinal András, but to the treasure-bearing Zsigmond. Besides the treasure, Zsigmond saved his bride, Princess Krisztina, too, but not via his uncle's planned route, through Csíkszentdomokosi Forest, but through underground caves. They groped their way down to the cellar. It was good, suddenly quiet, so quiet Miklós heard his blood pulsing in his ears. He didn't want Juli to turn on the lights, they groped their way further in, as far as they could. Then stopped. He wanted to stand beside her a while, to feel her close to him. His eyes slowly made out a faint light, or perhaps his skin saw how Juli's face had changed, as though not her own, as though it had perched upon her, like a dragonfly upon the still surface of a river. He wanted to catch the glittering dragonfly but froze, he would only end up longingly groping in the darkness, like every night he longingly fluttered against a window of

gleaming stars. He took a step, then stood still, and synchron-
ized his breathing with hers. Though she desired the light as
little as he did, Juli automatically felt for a switch, flicked it,
and a gap-toothed row of neon tubes lit up. In the long, endless basement lay school benches from all ages, heaped one on
top of the other. In the back, between the wrought-iron
benches draped in dusty cobwebs were coat stands, their legs
ending in twisting creepers, as though they'd gone to root. On
the stands were fraying jackets, buckled overcoats, and old-
fashioned things, as though their owners had just stepped out
for an extended break. It was an astonishing sight. For a long
time, they had been searching for this place, and now here it
was, in front of them, they could touch it. It was puzzling it
took so long to find it. Here it was, something that embedded
their school in time, confirming their existence, too, something
important, more important than Ms Vízi's open lesson.

Completely forgetting himself, Miklós ran upstairs to
share the discovery with the others, with Big Tempfli, Little
Tempfli, and Pongrácz, who were forever talking about such
things, and Ligeti, whose grandpa was once headmaster. He
sprinted to the top of the stairs but at the doorway recoiled at
the bright light. He stood a while, dazzled. Then he got used
to the light but carried on standing agape. The extent to which
his classmates had tangled history was unbelievable. Because
what had happened was András Báthory had got nowhere
near to crossing the Carpathian Mountains, Voivode Mihai
hadn't been able to enter Transylvania, or rather he had, but
immediately fell captive when Misi Holl and Szikszai locked
him in the gym hall boy's changing room.

Comrade Caricas, who as a party member oversaw the school Youth Communist League, was keen to step in, but on the one hand, he didn't have the requisite historical knowledge, and on the other, he saw no outrage on his comrades' faces, but instead amusement. He correctly saw that the comrades were enjoying the performance, certain that the events were playing out in the yard so unusually to create a more dramatic finish. And also they hadn't a clue who was who. Their belief was that history was the fulfilment of the people's dream, so every skew-whiff, half-baked event would play out with dreamlike direction.

The only teacher possessing any historical knowledge was maybe Comrade Szilágyi, but he couldn't come to Mihai's aid either. The changing-room door was built of such wood and held by such hinges, it even held strong when Lányi's crowd tried to ram it down with a changing-room bench, when puny Császár locked them in, in revenge, for giving him a wet willy. Voivode Mihai first beat the door with his fists, then just made threats, and finally broke into tears. Sebe's father was a barber, he combed beautiful ringlets into his son's hair. And Sebe was liked by the teachers. When asked to recite in class, he got so nervous that sweat dripped from him, and his corkscrew locks were sodden through.

Miklós didn't budge. However, it wasn't the whooping Báthorys that so amazed him after all, but what he'd found in the basement. Not the clothes, not the age-old furniture, but what he glimpsed in her, in Juli. In the mysterious basement, he hadn't only cut through great gaps in time but had seen through her too, or rather had seen into her, and there his gaze had stopped. He had discovered her secret. She didn't keep it in her heart, which he saw, like his own, was just beating faster than usual; nor anywhere else, you see, the secret wasn't if she was a virgin, if she'd slept with anyone, Miklós didn't care. The one thing he wanted to know was if she would give herself to him. Yes, this he wanted to uncover. This was the secret. And this he still lacked. That is, it wasn't ready. Hence he was so scared, for it was up to them, himself and Juli, to make it happen.

They'll be fine, thought Comrade Szilágyi. He withdrew to the staff room. Inside were six teachers, the ones who didn't want to know and plainly signalled so; they can't see, they can't hear, because the Party Congress is coming up, and they're following the big rally on TV, full volume. The rest however were glued to the windows but craning their necks this way and that, when they realized, something had gone terribly wrong. Comrade Dulea's deputy was storming off. The schoolyard was silent. Normally, Arthur Caricas would shout so loud, everything fell into line, but he was too slow. Instead, from a window on the second floor came the quaking voice of Bereczki, the Class IX genius who could recite from university books: Incoming deaf-mutes! Yes, he alone saw Comrade Instructor Grigore, who had had countless run-ins with Miklós's crowd due to the common games court, where the deaf-mutes played handball and they wanted to play basketball, and so this evil, black-eyed man sent in his students, who scaled the fence, landed on the other side, and charged, crying inarticulate howls.

The game was over. At an astounding speed, the deaf-mutes' invasion solved everything, order was restored. That's to say, the yard emptied and the next lesson could begin.

Minutes later, in the director's office, the smoke was dispersing, as the school inspectors, examiners and Party comrades took their leave swiftly, their agendas having grown due to the approaching Party Congress. Teachers returned to their classrooms with their registers under their arms, and Sebe, released from the changing room, probably got top marks for his recitation in scientific socialism class. By the time the last bell rang, essentially nobody remembered a thing.

And yet, strangely, many things changed. First, the smaller court was opened into the big schoolyard, so the two schools were essentially merged, and consequently, the deaf-mutes could nip over whenever they fancied. And Miklós noticed that some pupils on hall duty patrolled the corridors with a partner who, rather than the red armband, wore a black tuft of hair pinned to their breast pocket. These black-foxtail-toting hall attendants weren't from the deaf-mute pupils but came from their own. One of these black foxtails was Lali Gózner, for example, who was a good basketball player, the best in the team, although there had always been something aloof about him, askew, you couldn't banter with him. Yes, this word, 'askew', was a keyword after the open history lesson. Gózner was from a poor family and was a boarder despite living in the city, but every week he turned up in a new chequered shirt, noticed by Miklós who was a fan of chequered shirts and was envious. And then there were Gulyás and Laczkovics, the roster of the black foxtail squad somehow took form unambiguously, and once formed, nobody contested its existence. These boys had more power than strength. They possessed unspoken privileges, it wasn't them that the school feared, nor them that it bowed and scraped before, but their unspoken privileges. Even the director, Vinkó, shook when he spoke to them, mind you, he always shook. Their movements were such, you couldn't look away as they crossed the schoolyard or the corridor. The black foxtails victimized the strongest, the bravest and the otherwise foolishly boldest, or rather, for example, Ernő Géza Nagy stopped in the school-yard and ordered someone at random to come to him, while the black foxes stood behind him, stood and waited, as Ernő Géza bit the victim's neck.

Miklós realized it was best not to get involved. He paid no attention. Whenever they appeared, he greeted them amic-ably, and always spoke first. He never looked at their breast pockets, never glanced at the fox tails. He was pleased as punch with himself for avoiding their snares.

During the summer break, he forgot about school too. When somebody asked who Eleonóra Vízi or Ernő Géza Nagy were, he blinked vacantly, spare him all this school talk. Every day he and Juli strolled to the banks of the Szamos River, where on a gentle slope Juli's family had an orchard. At the start of August, the water was low and the stumps of the old wooden bridge appeared, led to by a long sandbank that emerged from the river. The wooden stumps grew so hot under the sun that the swarming dragonflies couldn't bear to land on them. Miklós revealed to Juli that he secretly called her his dragonfly. Why? Because of the way you shimmered down in the base-ment, remember, during the open lesson. Did you know, asked Juli, the dragonfly is a predator, both its imago and its larva? The larva can even eat smaller species of fish.

Miklós said nothing. He plodded beside her back to the riverbank, deflated. Even she's bringing up school stuff! Imago, he'd never heard the word in his life. I hate school, he muttered, because he didn't like failing. Juli hadn't heard him. But the nice thing is, she continued, they mate in flight, in mid-air. And the boy holds the girl in his arms while she's laying her eggs. Isn't that nice?

As if struck by a bolt of lightning, Miklós realized that the inevitable event, for which he'd been waiting for months, was now going to happen. Juli, reading his thoughts, took his hand and set off towards their orchard. Miklós's heart was in his mouth, he felt he was levitating, floating above the ground. And in that elevating moment, he saw it reflected in the surface of the water, ah, nonsense, he just felt it on him: that distinctive foxtrot. For weeks now, he had been walking with that lilting, head-bobbing, shoulder-rocking walk. No matter what he thought, the black foxes had chewed themselves into everyone.

Translated by Owen Good

THe STORY OF MONeY

After learning through whispers that Ferenc had struck a vein
of gold I began optimistically wandering the world. When
I went to bed I would fantasize about finally buying the
neighbouring garden and building our own garden railway. I
couldn't understand why Ferenc wasn't happy, why his face
held so much pain, more pain than it could bear, and wherever
he went the pain dripped from his jowls.

Rozália often assured me I would inherit everything. But
what does everything mean? The gold! Give me the gold!

Ferenc's brother served twenty-five years in the Foreign
Legion and when he was discharged as a colonel he bought
ten per cent of the shares in Marseille port. When I was born,
a third of the shares were his and he was planning to become
the sole owner. He couldn't have come home but he often
wrote. In his letters, for reasons unclear to this day, he referred
to me as Little Pista. In photos he wore a black silk scarf, Antal
said he had a hole in his throat and when he wanted to speak
he reached under the scarf to cover the hole. Before his death,
he got married and it was his wife who informed the family
about the funeral. That was the last we heard. According to
Antal, he had his own island, like the If in Monte Cristo. If

you held the sea-scented letters to the light, you could make out the watermark of an enormous yacht. It had three masts, twenty-three swollen sails and a calligraphic monogram adorning the mizzen: 'A. L.' From the bulge of the staysails they clearly had good wind and yet this transparent boat was the epitome of uncertainty: Would there be a port somewhere, would there be wind in the days to come, would there be a newer percentage, five, ten, twenty-one, would you be able to plan, would minute follow minute, day follow day?

Ferenc didn't like my name, it was a pagan name, he said. István, for example, is a nice Catholic name.

Antal fabricated a treasure detector from a DIY magazine called *Handyman*. Our house was built in 1908 by Swabian masons. There was a copper boiler in the bathroom, a dishwasher in the kitchen, and the water was pumped from a ten-metre-deep well in the courtyard to the tank in the loft. In the seventies when the water pressure fell because residential districts were spreading like cancerous tumours, Antal put the tank back into use and hunted down the old pipe with the detector. Luckily he found it, nevertheless I continued hunting in secret. In case real treasure was hiding in the walls. Or in the courtyard. I dug out mugs, spoons, old coins, the courtyard became dotted with mounds like a graveyard. Paired with Antal's memories, the artefacts revealed a fantastic childhood—no small matter, but I was hoping for gold.

Let's dig Ferenc up! Dig him up!

Rozália didn't like money, yearning for money will only breed ill, she said. Rozália's father remarried when he was eighty. His daughters were angry at him, and he at his daughters. Before his death, Rozália and I paid a visit. I saw among the pillows a grey-moustached man and on the edge of the bed a small, fragile woman cupping her hand over his. According to Rozália, she married him for the money. Money can create desire where there was once abhorrence, can squeeze real tears from feigned grief.

Anna explains that her starting salary was three hundred lei. I was given twenty-five bani to buy myself lunch. One leu was a lot of money. Leu in Romanian means lion.

During the lunch hour, we went from school across to the cafeteria and fished in the aquarium with magnets for bani that had been flicked in. One hundred bani was equal to one leu. Bani in Romanian means money. With the bani we bought ice cream in plastic cups. Our history teacher said that selling ice cream in plastic cups was brought over from America by Ceaușescu.

Ildikó, citing that she was a girl, refused to put on my hand-me-downs. As a consequence of her rebellion she could afford a new uniform only once every two years. I hated the uniform, first it got bally, then shiny, and eventually a hole formed in the seat of the trousers. But that's not why I didn't like it. It stank and it made my skin itch.

At one time Antal was farming mushrooms in the basement, later his mushroom plot was relocated upstairs to the bathroom. We had enormous oyster mushrooms and for days we ate only mushrooms. As regular as clockwork the mushroom soufflé made me vomit. I even got a fever. I once ate twelve slices of apple pie at a girl's house and got a fever then too. The girl was mad for me. She only wanted to be with me. We went cycling together and as we rode down the embankment she came clean off. I laughed cheerfully, from which I understood that unlike her I wasn't really in love.

Lajos had grown a paunch by his middle age and it showed his good side too. But the money he continued to lock away from his sons. Heaps and heaps of gold and diamonds. According to Anna his legionary son had stolen the money from him, hence he was afraid to come home. Rozália once had Boriska do a card reading to find the fortune. Boriska came every Wednesday and sometimes read cards and sometimes coffee grounds. Instead of treasure she found a dead man in the cards. Must be József, Ferenc's younger brother, he hanged himself here in the loft.

We aren't being followed by death, added Rozália as an explanation, death lives with us. Sometimes I hear it scurrying about, like a mouse.

She said this and smiled. But why? Up in the loft, while inspecting the criss-cross of the joisting, I too always smiled. To this very day. And when I smile, sooner or later I think of death.

A few days later Ferenc died. While walking home from his burial I stumbled at the corner and from the procession headed to the funeral feast, István shouted: There's the treasure! Dig it up!

Rozália monitored Ferenc's affairs in the afterlife. Where he went, whom he met, what messages he had. He goes fishing a lot, said Boriska. Fishing? He didn't like fish, his whole life he was repulsed by fish.

Etelka's uncle came back from America. He was Edison's former business partner. In Budapest he founded a telephone company; he knew he was investing his money in the future. Guglielmo Marconi was nowhere to be seen yet, or at least he was still unknown, and this man already had the people of Budapest listening to radios. News on the hour and music between. He eventually shot himself for a woman, mind you, he was no spring chicken, that's to say, he would have died soon. He got a beautiful gravesite, we keep a photograph, a charming spot in the shade. The woman for whom he shot himself hadn't visited the graveyard once. The wife of whom he'd tired watered the flowers.

When we buried Rozália, I wondered whether Ferenc's coffin was still there. And inside the coffin what had remained? Just the bones? A handful of dust? I watched the gravediggers with fascination, the many things they must know. Had my father been a gravedigger . . .

Sándor was taken by the French woman to Lourdes, praying at the feet of the Holy Virgin five times in six months; they always sent a postcard, signed Sándor and Rose. Here our Rózsa similarly believed in miracles, after her own fashion, when she was diagnosed with cancer she treated herself with the leaves of her aloe houseplant. I made sure to water the orphaned aloes.

Let's talk about money, said Anna, you're a grown-up boy now, let's talk about it plainly and maturely like adults. There are some who need a lot, and some who are content with less, there are situations where the man handles it, and there are others where the woman does, it doesn't matter who does, as long as everyone's happy. Then you've nothing to worry about. Money can make you younger or make you older, it can drain you or fill you with apathy, there's no knowing, it all depends on the person . . .

We should talk about it, said Antal, but not brag about or flaunt our endless successes. In matters of money we Hungarians are bashful.

Bashful, bashful indeed, but aware that we can't live without it, hence you have to know how to treat money with care. Be clever and you'll be rich.

You can be rich without money, and you can be poor with pockets full of money . . . You can build a fence around your empire but what for? It's easy to get lost, forever building the fence higher, strengthening the defence with yet another ring.

Keep your wits about you, son, be mindful of who you have dealings with, but don't be untrusting, be courteous even if your partner has duped and deceived you.

Money doesn't bring happiness.

Yes, it does. The greatest of loves can soon die without money.

No, it doesn't.

Yes, it does.

Lajos's father-in-law built the town lido by the lake. Plane trees lined the pathway to the swaying boat restaurant. Unusually scented torches protected against mosquitoes, successfully. Night after night, many took amusement at The Torch Barge. What kind of fats are you burning, Károly, eh?

Károly had enough money to eat from a gold plate and whenever any 'somebody' visited his restaurant, he served them on the same. Because no man can be poisoned by gold.

Károly was a virtuoso, said Rozália, the Paganini of money! As every musical note was there in Paganini's violin, all the world's money found its way to Károly's wallet, to his safe. Or who knows where he kept it. Because he never had any money. Once he was broken into but they didn't find a single banknote. Nowt. He had no bank account either. Seven years after his death, when his son-in-law was buried in the family vault, it was said Károly's body still glittered golden, immaculate. And that's the truth, assured Rozália. He was as handsome as he was in his twenties.

I want to live forever. My future isn't ash and dust, and my past isn't youth. No one will be able to tell my story because they won't be able to see the beginning, the middle, or the end. I whisked through life without a worry, life for me is as much as a handful of air. My story will be told only when there are twice as many words as there are now, when sentences shorten and the sunlight shines through their bodies, when poets and writers are born who don't incessantly bind and weave plot threads but lose themselves in describing the sweetness and pain of eternally elusive ideals. For such artists, it'll be another century and a half of waiting.

The very first Károly, being the best wine merchant in the country, became Her Imperial Majesty Maria Theresa's purveyor and was ennobled as a baron. He had a reputation for being an avid collector and was brought watches from distant lands because he personally recompensed the strains of the journey with great honour. By his old age, he had gone dotty and walked around in women's clothing, his children and servants ordered to bow before him, addressing him as Her Imperial Highness. He broke the watches to smithereens and hurled them out the bedroom window, from then on he collected footwear. Károly's new self was a shoe fanatic.

Etelka explained that he was still living somewhere around St Petersburg. That is, he hadn't died. He had no self that could die. Or rather, he switched them up. There had been Jóska Ferenc, Miklós Horthy, Adolf Hitler, János Kádár and now perhaps Mikhail Gorbachev. He collected watches, then shoes, then stamps, then tea labels, then samovars, then chess pieces, or perhaps watches again.

Spring drove everyone mad. Father Mihály began spreading new doctrine in the church. He had heard about iconoclasts from Pál Szabó Nyárádi. There was no other explanation for the people's unexpected enlightenment than that the Saviour was secretly walking the Earth.

István, his younger brother, had mental cogs turning at the double. He was continuously whipping counts. But the counts didn't mind because they were none the wiser. The ink sizzled at the touch of his quill, and the parchment singed under the curves of his letters. Once he paid a visit to the battlefield to see it and experience it. Blue bodies lay sprawled about the earth, blue corpses, their enormous tongues swollen and dangling from the black pits of their mouths. Looters had stripped their corpses of everything, their wagons piled high with

fur-lined coats, scarfs, boot liners, amulet-shaped trinkets . . .
On their bodies were star-shaped holes, from some of which
there was still a thin trickle of blood. For days István's hands
reeked of corpses. He frequently smelled his hand as he made
notes of his observations. He had never written more meticulous descriptions, besides those of his personal property. In my
possession are the following: one round-cornered, extendable,
folding table (mint condition), one square sideboard, three
long benches (pine wood) to border a room, one peasant armchair, two waxed dining chairs.

According to Etelka, her father-in-law, György, was the richest.
From his property, an entire village could have been bequeathed
to every inheritor since, and there would still have been plenty
to hanker for.

György's wife was a famously stingy woman: a stingy
woman from a stingy family. György suffered as much as only
women did. Many times he rebelled, but this woman was the
kind who had a sense for what was coming, thus he could
never break free. After the birth of their first child, when she
understood the pain that came with childbirth, she never let
her husband touch her again. And so no more children came.

The woman didn't love György because he was a man and
because he was a Hungarian.

György's father-in-law sold the gold mines because he suspected that America would soon be discovered and so he
chose to invest his money in shipping. He bought the whole
of America from Columbus for a pittance. He could buy

anything. The reason he hoarded money was to be able to buy anything. More than once had he been sold the secret of life, and more than once had he paid the price, though he wasn't a gullible man.

The year György's grandchild died, paper money was invented.

Dream about fish, and you shall strike upon a gold vein. Dream about money, and you shall strike upon a shoal.

The money-fetish riddle is none other than the life-fetish riddle but made visible in a form that dazzles the eye. For example, if we were immortal, who would care about money? If we were immortal, this instant I would cut a slice from my stomach and shake out the ghastly pieces of lead, or simply toss the whole lot in the bin. Namely, we would daydream of death eternally and fetishize money's negative. Which would be the same as a money fetish.

As the seed is blown across great distances by the wind, so our ancestors, too, drifted to this place.

My ancestor is Taksony, his was Zoltán, his Árpád, his Álmos, his Előd, his Ögyek, his Ed, his Csaba, his Etele, his Bendegúz, his Torda, his Szemény, his Etej, his Apos, his Kadocsa, his Berend, his Zsolt, his Bulcsú, his Balog, his Zombor, his Zámbor, his Lél, his Levente, his Kölcse, his Ompód, his Mikse, his Mike, his Beszter, his Budli, his Csanád, his Bökény, he the son of Bondorfán.

Bondorfán's wild nature stood out among the rest, as did his unexpected sorrow. Why are you so sorrowful? I don't know. Something's missing. Something was there but now it's gone. Something's eating me inside.

It was difficult then to talk in Hungarian about sorrow's causes. The word 'melancholy' didn't exist yet. Nor did 'memory'. It was as difficult as portraying nowadays the passing of time, not in a novel, but in a short story a few pages long, furthermore knowing that time doesn't merely pass, it wears on.

Bondorfán defeated every Chinese dragon that dared draw near, and he could break in horses in the shortest time. He gripped the horse by the head with both hands, stared into the horse's eyes, and instantly could do with it whatever he pleased. From people, too, he warded harmful spirits. But he didn't know where to begin when he himself got the blind staggers. First, he went berserk, ran riot, and struck down anyone that crossed his path. No one could rein him in. Then he dropped to the ground and cowered for days without moving.

I must buy women!

He lay pursuit to the thought he had quashed many times before: the process of buying women was set in motion. And following a lengthy and arduous journey, they arrived in our country. Naturally, at that time our country wasn't our country.

Back then they gave one horse for half a dozen juvenile girls or two virgins fit for wifedom, for widowed but childless, well-toothed, firm-breasted womenfolk they gave two horses. Back then a whole country could be traded for a single horse, an immaculate, white horse.

Naturally, some people thought this price was high. Bondorfán had been swindled, they said, because they could have bought much better wares that were both closer and cheaper. And they might have been right.

Bondorfán, albeit he was our György's ascendent and not his stingy wife's, foresaw his approaching fate. He did rebel but without much conviction. And not a good spot, you say?! My ass! When he closed his eyes he saw a city on the banks of the Danube, at summertime, a fresh June summer, the asphalt yet to soften, still only blemished by the previous year's unfashionably high-heeled shoeprints, a smattering of pebbles, a coin, what have you, not yet the dog days, but in front of a bookshop, men and women already lounging under parasols, idly chatting, occasionally raising a beer to their lips. Bondorfán wanted to lift this moment out of the future and set it before his companions to show them. He wanted to utterly convince them.

Then of course the council assembled. Following a heated, vigorous row, Bondorfán's body was tied to horses and torn to pieces.

In Bondorfán's time, people rarely felt pain or joy. They pushed through their nameless days virtually unaware. But Bondorfán was different. He sought out joy, he dreaded pain. He didn't sleep for weeks because of a bad tooth until he mustered the courage to hammer it out.

Before the roaring waves of fear crashed down on his head, he fearfully turned back in time, and as though hopping atop wooden stakes, his figure skipped and shrank towards the horizon.

The father of Bondorfán was Farkas, his was Otmár, his Kádár, his Belér, his Keár, his Keve, his Keled, his Dama, his Bor, his Hunor, his Nimrod, his Thana, his Japheth, he the son of Noah.

Etc. etc. Until the destitute, empty and sad beginnings. To nothing.

The world can be described in ninety-nine sentences. One of them is about money.

Translated by Owen Good

Loneliness

If the man perching on his elbows in the third-floor window didn't know the woman in the green dressing gown and wanted to learn her name, he could go down to the street and pick up the envelope that fell from her rubbish bin, but things being as they are, he can spare himself the effort. Instead, perhaps he can stare at the soft towel folds of her dressing gown, or note the snatches of song filtering down from the fourth floor, or simply carry on idly gawking out the window, in which case the sealed letter remains unread, because that miserable bin hoker who will pick it up the next day stuffs it into his creaking handcart to bring it with the rest of the paper to a waste collection point on the edge of town, where it's shovelled onto the back of a tipper lorry, dumped barely two hours later into the chlorine basin of the paper factory in Réce, and eroded to smithereens in seconds by obliterating whirlpools, in short, the bin hoker known as Gyuszi can't read, even if he did finish his eight grades in Elementary School No. 10.

Her worsening headache may have caused Ildikó Halász not to notice the envelope tumbling over the edge of the bin. Were it not for her sore head, she probably would pick it up, not to open it and read it, but because in all her born days she was a neat and orderly soul. The unopened letter might seem a contradiction, but it stands to her defence that the sender, marked with a red stamp, a cooperative that recently began experimenting with granting loans, sent her five letters in under a month. Ildikó is too pedantic, which is probably why she has such frequent headaches. The windows don't close properly and even though she cleans from dawn till dusk, when she goes to the toilet at night her soles are black with dust. Moreover, she inhales the dust, and this is no ordinary dust, you need only look out to the western end of the town where, in the form of a terrifying black cloud, you'll see Giroban Holding Group S.C., who can manufacture Europe's cheapest tyres because they spend diddly-squat on filtration systems. Black rubber dust is more harmful than cement dust. It's second only to ammonia in harmfulness, so she might consider herself lucky that a long time ago the fertilizer factory was built in Târgu Mureş rather than here, despite a certain Comrade Dulea pulling all the strings to that exact purpose, himself being the top man of the town's Party Committee and the provident father to two chemistry undergraduates. During the night Ildikó had a dream, and now, standing at the edge of the pavement, the dream is vividly coming to life in her head, indeed it's as if the dream is being projected onto the wall of the opposite apartment block, she can plainly see the scene, as she is escorted down a long, steeply sloping underground corridor, and what's more, into prison, she can see it now, deeper and deeper they go, and when she looks back the world above glimmers in a window as small as a single brick. But why she has been locked up, whether there's been a hearing or a sentence and whether she's committed some sort of crime aren't revealed in the dream, or at least none that she can recall.

Another contributing factor to her headache is that Ervin Zakk has just left her place, who, despite being fifteen years her junior, frequently pays her visits, what's more, he often stays until dawn, or perhaps for breakfast, as has occurred the last few days in particular, even though there's nothing between them, Ildikó often fantasizes of intimately 'receiving him' one day, like—and here usually follow many variations on the same simile, but which often describe the meeting of a simple household object, a coin, soap, a sword, a flashlight, with one of the elements of nature, mostly earth or water.

Ervin is thirty-five years old and works at a newspaper where a new editor-in-chief was recently appointed. The new editor-in-chief doesn't hate Ervin as much as the former did, and so Ervin thinks the time has come for him to be promoted to columnist. With that consideration he descended on Pista Tavi, who as the father-in-law to the rival paper's editor-in-chief was president of the publishing board, too, meanwhile naturally he was also in politics, or if not politics, then the tangle of public life surrounding politics; but more simply put; the new editor, from the bottom of his heart, hated this man 'like scabies'.

Next to her headache, suddenly Ildikó's other ear begins to whistle. The right one. The left first piped up when Ervin grunted at her, 'shift your arm over.' Incidentally, it was a harmless sentence, as was Ildikó's compliant movement away, however, if they had reached that point, if their elbows had accidentally met, she had expected an entirely different reception. Perhaps, that Ervin might caress her hair, or cup her fingers and press a kiss into her palm. But instead he growled and nodded his head, almost flicking her arm.

In Ervin's school days, like many of his classmates, he had a season ticket to the theatre. Back then the more decent-minded teachers would collect for season tickets to support the theatre, 'the spoken Hungarian word' (or as Ervin's overly zealous literature teacher would say, 'the oralized arts'), which, as it happened, was already supported by the state, to provide something for more decent-minded teachers to support, and so they wouldn't support something that wasn't to be supported. Ildikó Halász played the leading role of Eve in Imre Madách's *The Tragedy of Man*, and during one Sunday matinee school performance, in Scene Eight, the Johannes Kepler scene, she had revealed, or rather denuded her right breast. The following Sunday, in the company of his season-ticket-holding grandparents, Ervin returned to watch the show again because in opposition to his classmates he was adamant that the strap of her slip had fallen merely by accident, which, however, during the repeated visit, proved false. Now, a full twenty-two years later, Ervin would have had the opportunity to investigate that right breast more closely. He did have a certain interest but he was still hesitant, because the subject on which he was questioning Ildikó somehow made it improper, as it concerned the very same breast, indeed, it concerned its counterpart, the left one, too. Ervin wanted to find out whether Pista Tavi really had been the organizer of the orgy held on Labour Day in an orchard above the town behind the fences of the Forget-Me-Not Restaurant. Were the orgy to be revisited, 'made public' as the press would say, in detailed documentation, it would most certainly contribute to the downfall of Pista Tavi and furthermore of his son-in-law, or more precisely, to breaking the rival paper's rise, and feasibly to Ervin's promotion.

It's not as though the public didn't know the tiniest details of the orgy at Forget-Me-Not, even that Comrade Secretary Marika Bodoki had planted her blue silk knickers, deemed by many to be imported from France, though they were merely wares of the nearby Casin lace factory, albeit manufactured for export, onto Comrade Dulea's whatsit, and flew them like a flag atop a flagpole. But of course, it's one thing to know something and another to read the same in the paper blow by blow.

The next moment Ildikó had all but told him everything, or had reached a point where, if Ervin's hand had touched her breast, either one, she would have divulged everything about that breast, and then about its counterpart, too, in other words, she would have left absolutely nothing untold.

Holding her rubbish bin, she waits on the kerb in the not overly heavy but neither insignificant traffic to cross to the rubbish shed. The sun is setting, and Ildikó knows no place on earth scarier than the gloomy shed. In the dark at least she won't see the scurrying shadows, or feel a pang of conscience when she essentially dumps the bin's contents at her feet in the lee of the apartment block wall. Now, however, it isn't her fear of the shadows that hinders her from crossing, the paralysis arrives in her legs from somewhere much farther afield, from a distant space, better put, a distant time, to put it best, not in her legs but in the nerve tracts that control the muscles, but what arrives isn't paralysis because that's at most a secondary symptom to the confusion that causes one's nerve tracts to freeze like overloaded wires incapable of transmitting the information. Yes, in Ildikó's brain, a moment from the past is virtually exploding, this is causing the neural block. Ervin, arguably, brought about the explosion because if he wasn't the one to plant the bomb, he was the one to light the fuse. Yet the explosion isn't a real explosion either, or it is an inversion of one. To Ildikó, it is akin to the feeling of finding the crucial word while doing a crossword, though not quite to that, but to the feeling after, when having successfully solved the puzzle, she triumphantly tosses the paper aside and is suddenly consumed by the emptiness of the idle and lonely evening, and can't summon anybody unto whom she can foist this state now crashing down on her. Now, however, she knows that Ervin must be responsible, yet as she thinks of him, instead of his face, she sees Pista Tavi's, and that famous evening, in that famous restaurant, still known to all as Forget-Me-Not, which is of course absurd because who wouldn't want to forget. And the fact that the restaurant is known as Forget-Me-Not in Hungarian, Nefelejcs, is also quite absurd because really its registered name is Romanian, Număuita, after all, our story is set in Romania, yet everyone in the town, from among those in our story, even the Romanian Comrade Dulea, speak Hungarian, which, however, here and now, bears no significance whatsoever. It was a memorable evening, as before it she had hoped that finally she might get past something which, from then on, she wouldn't have to fear, and at that time it was the fear she wanted to be rid of most, at least as much as the coarse hair that grew on her legs, or a wrinkle at the corner of her mouth, even though she had a gut feeling that the fear's dissolution, of course, wouldn't better her condition by much, because that fearful self would be lost, but in return, she would get the roles that were still being given to Böby Derzsy, the most talentless actress on the planet. At the time, naturally, these soirées weren't called orgies, but 'burger nights', which of course could mean that burgers, that's to say, meatballs were eaten, but alas that's not what it meant; detailed summaries were provided by the waiters, the chauffeurs, the actors, the actresses, even the comrades themselves illustrated the minutiae during their coffee breaks, and so the secretaries forwarded this on, including to their hairdressers, and amid the distortion of hair dryers, the hairdressers spread it like an epidemic, like mumps, for instance, which for adult men who didn't contract it as children can be exceedingly dangerous, hence whenever there's a case of mumps in the nursery, every son-bearing mother feels it is vital to pay a visit to the sick child and have her own kiss them, while she, of course, can tell the fellow mum the latest details of the 'burger night'. The 'burger night' always began with brandy and was concluded when Pista Tavi ordered the underwear off every comrade, male or female, where applicable, and finally smashed Laji Rupi's current violin over Jani 'The Blockhead' Derzsy's head, so that upon it, that is, upon the violin, for the rest of time, nobody could ever play Rupi's gorgeous song that started: 'The nest of the great reed warbler . . . ' Ildikó bottomed a glass of brandy which knocked her out, and she became a sack of potatoes, while oddly her consciousness cleared and she was alertly watching from inside her own inert body, though such inertia didn't bother Pista Tavi, he shoved her into a semi-dark pantry, had her kneel in the corner, held her head with one hand, while the other unbuttoned his fly, back then zippers were still rare, started effing and blinding, perhaps because for some reason he could only whip out a tiddler, but he soon became more menacing, and the thought occurred to poor Ildikó, still alert, that there really was nobody on this planet who would protect her. But only the following day at noon, after she had gone home to the actors' dormitory where she still lived then, all the more so as in the part of town named Major where her present-day flat stands there grew orchards of fragrant peaches, after she had stood under the shower in the dormitory bathroom, and after from under her breasts, from the crease under her right breast, there broke forth that sickening Pista Tavi smell, only then did she throw up. Since then, she throws up regularly. Most recently, just a few days ago, she awoke to the feeling that she was going to vomit and swung open the window in case it helped because she often had terrible bouts of retching, from the bottom of her womb, and she didn't want to wake up the neighbours again, the wind blowing above the dark town, she leant out the window and soon felt better, yet as she turned back, the condensed Pista Tavi smell hit her nose, at which she immediately reproduced her first portion of dinner.

She should have got revenge. She would have had a chance once, during that famous Christmas when that glorious regime's people bit the dust, that's to say, periodically so, but soon they were on their feet. Today the most she can do is satiate the curiosity of a scandal-hungry journalist, which she would be delighted to do, but when she starts talking to Ervin about Pista Tavi, his face appears where Ervin's face should be, and it's Ervin's face she wants to see because she likes this face, this cheerful and young face, on which, even late at night, the lines chirpily answer back to the shadows of fatigue, and when dawn comes, they immediately spill about, and within moments, gleefully smoothen. She's in love with the boy and thinks about him night and day, hoping and praying that he'll be loved by everyone. And she tells everyone, because she enjoys talking about Ervin, how clever he is and well read, composed and pure, beautiful and innocent. It's such fun to toy with him! Whew, you fell for that one, kiddo, she often says, or, that'll get you scratching your nut sack, in short, they casually pull each other's legs as children might, and then enthusiastically plan their joint theatre piece . . .

Now, she suddenly sees herself from the outside, as though she were perched on the willow tree standing at the corner, or peering down from a window, perhaps switching places with the gawking man, if only for a few minutes. Maybe he deserves it, the gawking man, for five minutes to feel Ildikó Halász's aching head, standing in a green dressing gown at the kerb holding a rubbish bin, not to mention, while someone is watching. The man leaning in the window has been looking the other direction for a while, he was counting the lights turn on across the way, and now he's watching the body of a bird crushed against the grey road, as the wind lifts its ragged feathers, except there's not a breath of wind, at least not in the treetops. Later he'll lose himself in the night sky, he'll gaze at the moon and the stars, and thus be oblivious to the swarms of Pista Tavi–faced monsters and see nothing of the lonely woman's fear, though according to the code of chivalry, the man ought to stomp a foot in the direction of the monsters to make his presence known, and if necessary, to rise to the defence of the weaker sex; besides, he doesn't much like Pista Tavi either, and will read at the bottom of the article about the Forget-Me-Not orgies with pleasure and satisfaction that Pista Tavi has resigned as secretary, mind you, afterwards, he will learn of Tavi's appointment in Strasbourg with absolute indifference; just as the next morning, when fairly indifferently, at most shuddering at the event's proximity, he clutches at the green towelling which, like the bird, is plastered to the asphalt, a dark-red stain surrounded by fluff. Ildikó, meanwhile, has looked down from above and found herself again, that self who knows how far she is from Ervin loving her. Despite the falling dusk, she does see that her hair is thinning, her hairdresser's not so talented, and then that the crowns on her teeth are wearing down, they need changing but she hasn't the money, she isn't getting parts in the theatre, she does do one-off gigs, but ever more seldom, she put together a few simple little shows and takes them to school and nursery fetes; at the most recent she recited Sándor Petőfi poems on the anniversary of 1848, at the next she's reciting Endre Ady's poem 'Ifjú szívekben élek' at a high school speech day. She has a flat in a housing block, she has her mother's savings deposit with the smattering of money that her mother gathered for her own burial, and her dresses are all worn, in short, she can't see how she can change her life, but she senses that if she doesn't change something now, it'll be the end of her. She's clinging to Ervin, but he's becoming ever more selfish and hysterical.

And perhaps were something more intimate to develop between them, how long would it last? How long? Ildikó's fifteen-year-old self appears before her, a slender, brown girl in white knee-socks and a blue pleated skirt on her way to the Labour Day parade, and she imagines Ervin there with her, but he was still only a baby, so how about Zsuzsi's house party

when Bandi Szepesi and she locked themselves in the bathroom, and she let him take her virginity, she imagines Ervin
instead of Bandi, she thinks what they might have said to one
another then, how the balloon-headed, blond, barely three-
year-old boy would've reacted, how he would have stuck his
little fingers into her body.

She stands at the side of the road with a dizzying headache, waiting until she can cross to the other side. The bin is
now so heavy that her right shoulder is almost hanging a
full span lower. As though she was carrying a dismembered
corpse, at the very least. She would be caught of course,
though there are always discarded bones and less identifiable,
nauseating odds and ends strewn about the bins. Yes, during
that revolutionary Christmas, it had crossed her mind to grab
the kitchen knife and to call on Pista Tavi, to shove his
screeching wife to one side, which was unlikely because it was
well known his wife was half-a-head taller and fifty kilos
heavier, then to charge to the armchair in front of the TV, to
stab the knife into Pista Tavi's heart, who would accept the
knife with resignation, as though a revenge-hungry revolutionary had stepped right out of the screen. For twenty-five years
she's been living with Pista Tavi's corpse, carrying it everywhere, she had a corpse for a husband, for her lovers and for
her aborted child, for a director, every partner, the bus driver,
the truculent taxi driver.

What sacrifice has she not made? Her whole life was a sacrifice. Defeat, loss, failure, that's all it ever was. That evening
she had decided, if it must be so, she would turn Pista Tavi's
head, but he didn't so much as look at her, moreover, when
she timidly made an introduction, saying, have you noticed,

comrade, your name is Tavi, like a lake, and mine is Halász, like a fisherman, to which Pista Tavi dimly asked, what's there to notice? That was when she drank the brandy, that moment.

Darkness slowly falls. The headlights of the passing lorries create endless shadow figures, as though they were being peeled from her body standing at the roadside, now a donkey, now a goat, now a poised chamois, its hooves packed together into a palm's width, and then they scurry off among the blocks but carry on peeking from behind the concrete walls. Ildikó recognizes them as one by one their heads are carved out of the darkness by the beams of light. Yes, she should have called on Pista Tavi then, during that clear, snowless Christmas, when for three days a warm south wind blew across the town, and carried the rubber dust far away. She should have at least spat in his face, but it would have been enough to get a look at him, to say to him, well, Comrade Tavi, how's it hanging? She still could have got in then because his bodyguards returned on the third day. And today, if by some stroke of luck she got in, she would find a feeble, blank-faced and sick old man, a shred of a man, more evil of course than ever.

Ildikó stands on the kerb and counts the lorries trundling by. Or rather not the lorries, but just repeats the number plates in her head. What for? She doesn't want to stop time and doesn't want to let it continue either. But not to worry, she thinks, at least it's dark now, she can cross to the rubbish shed and freely dump the bin's contents at her feet. But it's been dark for a while. In the nearby barracks maybe the soldiers are   leaving for their nighttime shooting practice, perhaps they're practising a top-secret night drill. Perhaps the passing lorries aren't real. The pain in Ildikó's head is becoming more unbearable. She thinks of turning back, going to the flat, calling Ervin, declaring that she has more on Pista Tavi, that she urgently wants to share her information, but she'll only give it up if . . . But then something pops in her head; her rounding eyes acknowledge: the pain has vanished. It happened so suddenly as if it was a sign. The sign that encourages her not to go back, to leave that blessed Ervin be, to forget everything, to start a new life, to get back on the stage, to play the parts she never played, to play them as only she can.

Translated by Owen Good

BeFORe MIDNIGHT

A friend asked for my help, to work out what dark scheme had plunged him into life-threatening peril. He explained that it all began with a runny nose. How he was both touched and of course revolted when Kati (the owner of the nose) threw her arms around his neck and smeared his jacket. Lowering her voice every time she glanced towards the neighbours' flat, he suspected she'd had another falling out with her cotenants. My friend suggested he give her a lift to the university, expecting that she would prefer to walk in the fresh air, but she leapt up, smiling, and pressed a grateful kiss on his cheek.

He was so delighted that it's no wonder he doesn't clearly remember what happened later. Most probably he offered to wait for her in front of the university and then to drive her home, perhaps stopping somewhere for a cup of tea on the way, Kati, however, asked him if he wanted to listen to an interesting lecture. My friend nodded with a smile because he hoped she would take him to her own class, perhaps he even asked what the class would be, and even though it was completely beyond him (Ankersmit's historical representation), the topic excited him, as did the chance to be a student again. But no, she didn't invite him to her lecture; in the corridor she approached a short old man and after a few hushed words beckoned my friend over, entrusting him with a wave of her hand to the man, but then disappeared around the corner.

The grey, wizened man silently ushered him into a poky lecture room where almost every seat was occupied. So he, that is, my friend was forced to take a seat in the front row.

The old man took his seat at the table in front of the board, pointed to my friend and announced that he had invited someone to speak about the Hungarian composer Béla Bartók. Only then did my friend realize where he had wound up: for the man addressed his students not in Hungarian, but Romanian, making it plainly clear that these students sitting around him were students of the Romanian Department. They gave my friend a cold stare. This coldness could hardly have been his fault, as he hadn't uttered a single syllable yet, though naturally, they might have been offended by his mug alone. Many wouldn't so much as look at him; tapping at their phones under the desk.

My friend laughed and stood up to take his leave, citing an obvious misunderstanding, but when he spoke, to his surprise, he glibly strung the foreign words into sentences and it was such a pleasant feeling that he spoke all the more, and fluently, like in a dream. He didn't get lost among the winding grammar or rhetoric and so suddenly found himself speaking on the topic, that is, on Béla Bartók. He even knew the Romanian name of Bartók's birthplace, what's more, he remembered the ethnomusicologist who named the Hungarian composer 'the Romanian people's truest friend'. He spoke about Bartók's music artfully, impartially, even feeling a temptation to hum the melody of a Colindă used in Piano Concerto

No. 3, but taking into consideration that he was delivering a lecture to historians, he plumped for the human determination, and to demonstrate the sort of man Bartók was, turned to the period following the First World War. He would speak about the unjust partitioning of Hungary, he thought, including the loss of territory to Romania, as objectively as he might about the country's later descent into fascism, then when analysing the reasons for Bartók's voluntary exile, he wouldn't spare the bumptious Hungarian politicians, nor the scholars and writers who had strayed from the flock. But he didn't make it that far. The teacher, who most resembled a police clerk hunched over his desk, interrupted, requesting him to talk about Vianu Dan (or Diana Vad), as one couldn't discuss that period without mentioning the name. Giu Vlad did also play an important role, interjected my friend, about to move on when in a raspy tone the paunchy little man corrected him, reiterating the unfamiliar and thus elusive name. My friend felt exactly as he had, back in the day, being forced to sit an oral exam in scientific socialism, known as sci-soc, a discipline without even a minimal bearing on reality.

Noticing he was uncomfortable, the students immediately burst into activity and started shouting as if at an outer-district flea market. Several threw clouds of torn paper in the air, or rather not in the air, but straight in my friend's face. One of the older women in headscarves (there were at least three in the room), who was certainly over fifty, mind you since the new pension law a fair few mature people have returned to university, springing from her chair, stepped up to him and shook her fist, yelling that the Hungarians had always treated Romanians unfairly. My friend, as if attacked by a dog, didn't look the woman in the eye. But a number of young men had now surrounded him, so he had to look somewhere. One had a gold ring in one ear, another's watch was gold. Fashionable, ribbed polo-necks hugged their chests, hideously expensive phones hung around their necks, and their bodies swaggered from side to side as if trying to reach some vulgar climax. It crossed my friend's mind that he ought to reach for his own phone because he had heard that in the event of an attack, this movement would take the assailant by surprise, though he felt this whole situation was ridiculous and totally unfair, he had nothing to be afraid of, never mind ashamed, he would get through it, whatever happened.

Softly, like a puffball mushroom, the old teacher gave a cautionary cough.

Seizing upon the new silence, my friend gathered his nerves and launched into quite an aptly worded speech. He doesn't deny the injuries done but today we have a great opportunity to take an honest look around and see that in our continent the countries that have gone the farthest are those where the actors of old have left the stage. He cited a few foreign examples, mentioning that he understood the question well because recently he had been to the West several times where he saw that the wounds had been successfully healed. His advice to everyone is . . . But again he was cut off by the professor who, signalling the end of the lesson, stood up and dashed out of the room like an impatient alcoholic. A few sped after him, and my friend wanted to leave too, but as soon as he moved the circle grew tighter.

This happened the same week as when in neighbouring Ukraine, the people took to the streets, shouting that the elections were rigged. Here, too, in Romania it was campaign time, and in Hungary a referendum was being held on dual citizenship. Contention can be famously contagious, and in the widespread tension, fighting can easily break out. Yet I know my friend well enough to say that he can avoid such situations. In the room, though, he panicked.

He could only free himself by violently yanking his arms. Stumbling, he made it into the corridor where he practically ran for the exit. He very nearly knocked over a pregnant woman as he passed through the revolving doors.

Cross and mortified, he got in his car to wait inside. He sat for some time but to no avail. And then it occurred to him, probably she had gone to collect him from the lecture room, and, upon finding it empty, had waited for him at the entrance, by the porter's room: she was a rational and logical woman.

He got out and made his way along the alley of thuja conifers towards the university building. It was misty, autumnal weather, by six o'clock it was completely dark. He saw nobody, yet felt as though he was being followed. The long and dark alley's silence seemed to grow more menacing, he quickened his steps, meanwhile, with his neck stiff as a poker, he listened behind him. Perhaps this was why he didn't hear the people coming opposite whom he only noticed when they were already towering in front of him. And since he was walking as quietly as possible, and since the alley was as black as a tunnel, the approaching group didn't notice him either and simply sped over the top of him.

Intent? Hardly. Even the antecedents, the students' unpleasant behaviour, offer us little reason to think this was intentional. Intent would suppose an overly calculated act of diabolical planning. And, besides, what would be the purpose? Revenge? Why? My friend is an unremarkable man, a musician in a provincial orchestra where no one wants to take his place (the shortage of musicians reached a bitter low when a one-armed musician was hired to conduct). They unintentionally knocked him to the ground and tramped across him like a sandbag in their path.

He got a scare but was otherwise fine. However, he didn't want to go into the building with muddy clothes and a mucky face, so he went back to the gate. When he noticed several people waiting for the bus, he stole behind a thuja conifer and started cleaning his face and clothes.

He was most annoyed that his plans had gone down the tubes. But he never has any luck. As soon as something nice is on the cards, he's bound to get a toothache, get lost, get called in for rehearsal, or the revolution breaks out. When pressed for an explanation, he believes that his greatest fault is being unable to let go of his envisioned future. He's going to tell me something personal because he realizes that the scourge is brought upon him by dark shadows in his own soul. Or not, there are no shadows, it's just his imagination is faulty. He'll explain what he means. Not long ago, he saw an Antonioni film, and he identified the film's two lovers with Kati and himself. Yes, there's no point in hiding it, especially now he's asked my help, he assumed that everything that happened on the huge snow-white bed in the film, had happened to them, too.

Even the porter had gone home, a lock had appeared on the iron gate. The building's windows bounced the light of the passing cars' headlights back like black mirrors. A light was still burning on the ground floor, and my friend went on hoping until the penny finally dropped: the neon light in the porter's room would be on all night. And my friend had damaged his phone, he couldn't call for help.

Suddenly the Moon came out and the garden was illuminated. Overhead a pair of turtle doves were roosting on a branch, huddling up together. A cruel arrangement. He was shivering from the cold and more than anything wanted to tell her about his ordeals. He was greatly reassured by the knowledge that there was still a runny, red nose and that he was in an intimate relationship with this nose. He set off in search of some means of exit but the fence couldn't be climbed. In one corner of the building luckily he found an open side door, he groped his way down to the basement, from where he came out onto the ground floor, and then walked along one of the wings of the U-shaped building, to the far side, and climbed out a window onto the street. The bus was just pulling in, and though he didn't usually take the bus, he got on, but stood, waiting for the bus to loop back to the campus entrance.

The street lights weren't lit but the wet asphalt was glistening delightfully in front of the bus. After the bend, he spotted his car but then turned to check if he could see the cross of the church on the main square. For years he had been terrified that one day it'd be stolen. Who wouldn't be afraid of such things in their hometown when it was filling with more and more unfamiliar faces? He was gaping out the back window when the bus stopped, opened its doors, and the rubber edge of the door crushed him against a vertical pole. The pain was like he'd been cut in two. He was unable to breathe and naturally to cry out either.

He survived, but could only get off at the next stop, in front of the buffet opposite the station. Droves of people were loitering on the pavement holding glass bottles. He was worried they would pick a quarrel with him but they didn't even notice him, or rather, they looked right through him, like a pathetic wretch teetering on the edge between life and death. He made off along the long avenue towards the university. There were fewer people here, and he mused on his situation. He patted his aching chest, but as he repeated Kati's name to himself, syllabifying it for a little sol-fa practice, the word alone brought him comfort.

After getting into his car and glancing at the dashboard, he was stunned to see it was past eleven and so decided he'd rather go home. The decision put him at ease, in fact, it was as though the city, too, breathed a sigh of relief; electricity reached the wires above and the street lights lit up. But no sooner had he arrived in their neighbourhood than he had second thoughts, and knowing how late Kati usually stayed up, he drove to hers after all, again with such excitement that he couldn't dodge the potholes.

The light was on; his courage restored, he parked in front of the house and rang the bell.

Reluctantly, he greeted the neighbours who were sitting in Kati's, full of the joys of spring. As always, they were leading the conversation, which for my friend went hand in hand with tedium and an unbearable itch. When he heard off-key notes, he also got an itch, the area varying in size depending on how off the note was.

Kati didn't even ask where he had disappeared to. My friend grew stiffer in the armchair and sank ever deeper into his eddying silence. From the conversation, he picked up on some kind of awkwardness that he couldn't put his finger on. He felt they were hiding what they had been discussing before he arrived, except their every word and gesture related back to it. Kati flushed red, whooped with laughter, and at her hairline, her forehead glowed amber. Her behaviour was unsettling, but my friend still found one thing that reassured him. And this was her face. Never had he found her more beautiful. Less beauty than an untouched snowfield, less snow than the joy and freedom of life. And less a face than a door, open or not, there it was in front of him. He wouldn't hesitate for a second if someone called out to him: Come on in, come inside, but know that there's no going back. He'd be through it in a heartbeat.

My friend stared at her face which was glowing brighter by the minute and started hoping he could finally tell her about his ordeals. He would show her his aching chest. Meanwhile, as he daydreamed, his heart was almost bursting with excitement. But suddenly he discovered a dark story written in the neighbours' hints, Kati's laughter, and the flicker of her eyes. It was a mess, deletions, corrections and scrawls, beginning to end. He used his imagination to fill in the illegible parts, like when he read a contemporary score. From the complex sketches and the triumphant, cocky symbols there blared forth a piece of music so simple it was almost banal. The picture cleared: a man had broken in on Kati, kicked in the door, drunkenly grinned and made filthy propositions, but hadn't stopped there, he had started to force himself on her. Why laugh about such a thing? My friend grew light-headed, his stomach lurched and he ran to the bathroom. Weakly, he

plopped himself on the cold bath edge, leant forward, and listened with his forehead pressed against the door. Now he
heard a different story, more terrifying and nauseating than
the first. It involved a man about whom Kati had been crying
that very morning. In other words, it wasn't the neighbours
she'd been upset about. Indeed, they did have a disagreement
but held no anger, certainly no hatred, after all, if they hated
one another nothing would ever change, so the man had
rushed off and later sent a bunch of red roses. (Oh, my friend
only just understood what that sneaky light in the room and
that stomach-turning smell were. Now he understood why
Kati's face was sparkling and her skin had a reddish glow.)
The man didn't have the roses delivered but brought them
himself, patiently biding his time in front of the locked door,
until Kati arrived home from university. Later the neighbouring cotenants also arrived, and Kati and the man were acting
very curiously, at which all of them had been chuckling
merrily since. The neighbours were only sorry they hadn't had
a camera. Embarrassed, Kati introduced the man to them,
though they know him well, Kati wasn't even on the scene
when they met him, mind you, they never had the pleasure of
meeting him with so few clothes on.

My friend then staggered out of the bathroom. Staggering
because as he was hunching on the edge of the bath, he
noticed a strange shaking. As though, down on the street, a
menacing crowd was approaching, moulded from the night's
muck, loudly trundling iron barrels in front of them. And so
reliving the day's most unpleasant moments, he involuntarily
began his escape, but too weak to say goodbye, he plopped
back in the armchair. Kati's face was growing more beautiful,

and more unattainable: it told him this door wouldn't open. The shaking became stronger, so strong, my friend was scared to stand from the armchair. As for how much of this is reality and how much is a product of his imagination? As is known, reality doesn't exclude imagination but installs it into its own machinery, and adjusts it so that in the end it's imagination that handles reality's own absurd affairs. It seemed ever more likely the next day might never dawn, which, namely, the undawning, did have advantages. He could no longer even begin to imagine that everything had happened with Kati on the snow-white bed. Hence he was happy to think there would be no tomorrow. Like this, all his problems were solved, he won't ask me any more questions, he doesn't care where the ominous shaking came from, or who's lurking in the shadows of these events, nor am I to investigate any further. Better he gets no concrete answer and the man remains unknown.

You know him, I interrupted and curtly left, not wanting him to stare.

Translated by Owen Good

MADHOUSE

'This lot are a pack of animals and are to be kept as such, well in hand,' snapped the institution's head consultant to Doc Haris, the intern huffing alongside him, as they hurried across the courtyard. Every word reached the understanding of Miklós who was lingering nearby, he sensed the supercilious eloquence of the words: 'as such' and 'well in hand'. He was outraged, meanwhile he really was acting like a dog on heat: he was hugging the tree trunk, thrusting his crotch against it, and whining.

Until 1948 the building had been home to the Greco-Catholic nursery school. The linden tree had remained from that time and owed its life to the school's closure: the teachers and nannies had wanted to cut it down as payback because the nursery children in their charge were forever hiding among its branches. Nearby the tree, another of the nursery's accessories was the low drinking trough whose vertically protruding rusting pipes hadn't produced a drop of water for years. And so, one could sit upon it happily, lifting one's face to the sun disc, as Uncle Lizard was wont to, a bony old man. Around him, basking in the dusty, sparse grass were his companions who were old and thin, too, their skin worn and red like scales.

Miklós's condition was coming along nicely, he rubbed against the tree ever more rarely. One day, having passed the baskers, he noticed Uncle Lizard's yellow eyeballs were following him. For days he'd felt Uncle Lizard leering at his back but now he'd got him! He spun around, leant forward, and started growling, then chasséing around the trough his barks grew more rabid as he snapped and snapped at the motionless old man who, losing his patience, eventually jumped down from the trough and confronted him. The others sprang up too and the many frail, old bones chased away the youngster, who once again collapsed in defeat.

He received yet another, different kind of sedative, and his referral was extended. The sedatives caused the dog to withdraw into the background and this helped his true self, albeit dully and wearily, to pull its way out of the deep. Tired, his limbs like lead, but still curious, he observed the yard's goings-on. Since he was a child, he was keen on fabricating explanations and theories, which was arguably why when the time came he applied for physics at university. He established that the truth lay with those who asserted that matter's impulses gained passage to the external world via human ingenuity. The headstrong lunatics who donned the costumes of this or that historical figure proved his theory: fallen out of time, in an attempt to compensate for their own costumes, they slipped into discarded ones. Yet more instruments of matter's vain time sickness. He came across two Napoleons which presented an opportunity for comparison. One captured the character purely in how he wore his hair, the other in how he held his hand. The first was perpetually fixing his wisp of hair, wetting it between licked fingers, and sticking it to his forehead, while the other signalled his status by resting his hand on his belly as he hypnotically marched back and forth a hundred times a day or more. But were someone to engage them in conversation, they could say nothing more than 'I am Napoleon, the great emperor, bow before me'. There were at least six Lajos Kossuths, the Hungarian revolutionary politician, but there were some Count István Széchenyis, too, which is interesting as the real statesman had spent a decent part of his life in a madhouse. They assumed a mask, like wearing a watch that didn't work and was merely drawn on. Even Jesus Christ couldn't string together a sentence, though a few months previous he'd taught Hungarian and French at Elementary School No. 10. Surrounded by vacantly blinking disciples, he strode across the yard and never stopped, so as he could convert those gone astray to the true faith with such power as would crack the stone trough in two.

The two Jesuses didn't fight because they both wore the same costume, nobody killed for that sort of thing. They were overtaken by aggression, like an occasional, unforeseeable eddy in the flow of matter. You could scarcely predict what caused their stunted lives to surge with such wasteful strength. They clashed, blood was spilled, but the nurses arrived and the scuffle was soon brought to an end. The nurses were never attacked and when the nurses dealt a beating, nobody hit back; they bore the blows at length with movements that flinched towards escape. However, if one of them took a bad turn, collapsed to the ground, foaming at the mouth, and jerked epileptically, that person was immediately pounced on, kicked, beaten with sticks, and stoned, as were the poisoned rats that staggered into the yard.

Doc Haris was upstairs, diligently making notes in the loft space. 'Existing therapies achieve nothing, or merely as much as stereotypes or occasional maxims further promoted in scientific literature.' He hated stereotypes and maxims because his boss, the head consultant, was forever reeling them off. 'What makes a commonplace a commonplace is the inescapable truth it bears,' this was the apex of commonplaces. Haris's dislike knew no boundaries, he was filled with disgust by the director's flabby figure and would have gladly tossed him out the window. He wanted to shake the head consultant in his cemented position and since the official cement seemed unbreakable; he was driving for some sort of great discovery. Hanging up his white coat, he went down among the patients daily and, taking inspiration from a John W. Croll study, examined how flexible these roles were, or how well the actors were able to apply themselves to other sorts of roles. He tried simple things. Rushing to Regent-President Lajos Kossuth, between breaths, he informed him that the emperor was abdicating the Hungarian crown and would enter into yet further conditions of peace, furthermore, as a mark of honour and respect, would hand over the throne to Kossuth. The politician nodded at the news, then, sinking into elegant thought, solemnly continued on his way, remaining the regent of all Hungarians. Doc Haris returned to his room disappointed. He hadn't been informed yet of Miklós's impulse theory.

Doc Haris lived in a neighbourhood of apartment blocks on the edge of town, and since he had no desire to walk home along the potholed, unlit streets, he wound up staying the night in the hospital's loft space. Maybe he didn't live in his suburban bedsit alone, and maybe he didn't want to go home for reasons other than the ankle-twisting streets—the next morning, there appeared at his office a young woman, younger than him, who arrived looking troubled and left puffy-eyed, but Haris continued to sleep at work. That afternoon he stormed out and returned later with a green suitcase and another two bulging paper sacks carried by the taxi driver. From then on, he never went anywhere. He obsessively made notes standing at the window, glancing down at the yard where the strollers' paths were inscribed in the dust so regularly, as if to be the calligraphic lettering of balanced minds, rather than of capricious madness. By then he was often joined in the loft by Miklós who had lately been complaining about his eyes, that's to say, his eyesight, thus each morning under the pretext of an eyesight test they engaged in lengthy colloquies. Miklós most enjoyed the cosiness of the steaming cup of tea and the early-morning sunshine which could transform the shabby yard into a freshly swept stage, where promising things would happen, and with this backdrop, even their aimless and rambling conversations felt more important. Miklós propounded his theory about matter's wandering impulses, of which Haris didn't understand a great deal, and diverting Miklós's conclusion, he repeated that it was precisely in their immateriality that the aimless and empty lives here differed from the aimless and empty lives in the outside world. 'When Ilonka is fucked from behind by Béla, neither produces a single drop of fluid. They know how to bite, how to smack, but the smack is aimed at nothing. Were an individual to be struck hard enough to be dazed, then their unconsciously collapsed body would instantly disappear from sight and be left in peace.' Doc Haris didn't think the adoption of historical roles was at all connected to time sickness, the explanation was less scientific than it was societal: it revealed an undeveloped sense of history. 'Essentially, within these nutcases, a one-million-year-old revolution is underway, but this revolution has never yet been victorious. The old consciousness cannot lose. But whoever discards their consciousness will find themselves.'

Miklós, intrigued, listened to Haris, who was led to this theoretical conclusion, which was hopefully a starting point for a new and different treatment of madness, by the great philosopher, the so-called madman, Nietzsche. 'The great thinker's insanity is no more than the casting off of the consciousness of conventions, swapping one's sheep-mind for one's true consciousness. We only see the madness, of course, the beastliness, the vacant role, yet the role is a folding screen behind which the person who aches to break free can spend their fury. This is the gist of my theory!'

Miklós was so touched by the speech that he glimpsed his own folding screen. Before his eyes were no longer mere blotches, that's to say, the blotches stopped floating, melted together, and covered the greater part of his field of vision: he saw out of his head as though peeping through a folding screen. This rather terrified him, yet his terror only bore further evidence for Doc Haris who was delighted at his ailment, 'aspis eye!' he named it, and immediately got out his head lamp and periscope.

He entered in minute detail what he'd found during the examination. The head consultant had been on his back more and more, 'forget the empty theories, people are rattled by all this global nonsense, don't you see, it's no wonder so many go crazy. But there's no place for quackery in this hospital. If they blow their top, then straitjacket, padded room or electroshock; if they have no symptoms, then they're pretending, kick them out, this isn't a sanatorium. Don't mingle with them, you'll go off your nut too. I hear you in the yard running messages as the French ambassador and talking to Lajos Kossuth. You mustn't mix things, Doctor. Leave history to the historians or the novelists.'

'It's not history I'm questioning, it's the sense of history that interests me, I'm examining its existence. It's a peculiar experience and those who partake in it to any degree, even under the effects of narcotics, can work out how to break their consciousness free from the power of the herd mind.'

The head consultant was preparing for his summer holidays and didn't want to get involved in anything. 'Write the symptomless patients' letters of discharge this week, so I can sign them. And let's send the pinscher home, I hear he's doing so well you drink tea together every morning. Do you sleep together, too, perhaps?'

What an animal, thought Doc Haris about his boss. Specifically a pig. Only interested in himself and only taking notice when the swill dish rattles. Capable of eating his own piglets if he was hungry enough. At the time, he had informed on his son for wanting to defect. That man informed on everyone. And yet now he's the Union Chair. At the first criticism, he kicks up a fuss like a sow who's seen the knife. And like a pig, there are plenty looking forward to his death and they'll have a jolly old feast at the funeral.

Miklós understood the light shining in his eye to be a friendly hand reaching out, and, as at the bottom of his eye

Haris espied 'the unquestionable symptom of apathetic conversion,' Miklós invited the light's warmth into the depths of his soul. Out in the yard, too, he saw his companions differently. He believed he had to give them some of this warmth, of this need for warmth, because they were sunbathing in vain, that's to say, besides sunshine's caressing warmth, the opening of matter was also essential. Just as a bare house wall might open to suck in, to ingest the old man leaning against it who has waited years for his loved ones.

Miklós liked to hide in the lee of the giant they called Bumbi; he enjoyed sitting beside him, as though in front of a house wall warmed by the sun. But one day Uncle Lajos Kossuth ate the nurses' sausages, Pimplenose's, and Forget-Me-Not's, who accused Bumbi and threatened him with no food for two days. This frightened Bumbi to death. Nobody ever dared lay a finger on him, nor the nursing taskforce known as the Three Graces, but by revoking his meals they could keep him in check like no other. Miklós had seen who pilfered the sausages, he went up to the nurses and told them to look round Uncle Lajos's mouth, his gob is pure grease. The nurses angrily shoved him aside, what nonsense are you spouting, Miklós protested, smell for yourselves who has sausage breath, to which again he was shoved aside, they never shied from physical means. All this being jostled was getting Miklós riled and he started growling. The nurses took out their syringes which mostly served to frighten patients but if necessary they'd jab anyone. Miklós got scared and was backing down when Bumbi stepped in front of the nurses and in a flash wrestled their weapons from their hands. They immediately became furious at which Bumbi lifted a heavy, wrought-iron bench over his head and prompted them to scamper. The two nurses scrambled to the corridor and soon returned with the Three Graces. These three hefty, neckless men could usually pacify even the most vicious patients. In their childhoods, their faces had already been flooded with the pure essence of hate. Peeling off the leather straps that crisscrossed their chests, they rushed towards Bumbi who'd already forgotten what had happened, he just stood there gormlessly, head down, and didn't dare look up. The nurses let him be, there was no punishment.

Doc Polyáki was filling in for the head consultant. This meant the nurses could kick their feet up all day, they tallied their winnings, divided them amongst themselves, and argued, or perhaps in complete agreement loaded the latest delivery into their cars. Polyáki was three years younger than Haris, yet he was the one appointed as ward deputy head. Perhaps due to his Freemasonry connections, perhaps because he was a committed churchgoer, meanwhile he had also lent advice to a minor but meddlesome politician; in any case, he had a few strings to his bow. Haris learnt of his colleague's promotion without so much as a peep, he later resolved that he wouldn't get into a conflict for something he inherently despised because then he would be the same as those he was fighting against. Polyáki, needless to say, wasn't suited for the job. He liked to torture the patients. He deprived them of their sedatives so that when they fell into a fit of rage he could come down hard, tie them to their bed or the hooks in the rage room, and then torture them with his personally designed instruments. Sin is a path to wisdom. He permitted nobody out to the yard, again to heighten tension.

Under these conditions, the patients started tormenting each other. Haris, jotting away in the loft space, believed that space deprivation alone didn't make them more irritable, or if it did, this further proved the existence of their herd consciousness. And the lack of any historical sense permitted the fury in their words, in fact, in the remnants and memories of their words, exactly as occurs during wartime; peoples slaughter one another along the front line of hackneyed ideologies.

Haris probably isn't right about everything, thought Miklós, who did witness the events more closely than Haris. In the basement canteen, even the smell changed when Bumbi handed over his secret reserves of sedatives to Anti, who otherwise would have ended up in the padded room, that is, with Polyáki and his innovative instruments of torture. With this gesture, Bumbi had come into his own, it wasn't merely in return for kindness, like when he lifted the bench, but his own stash. It was still within the possibilities of the herd mind, true, nevertheless, it was different, it was a mixture of things.

During morning tea, Doc Haris heard all about the incident, the power of the moment, and the new scent, which had better not get Miklós carried away because it would be risky for the researcher to change tac in his research after hearing such a report. 'Risky and rash, indeed, dear friend,' but as though to prove to himself that he wouldn't change tac, he continued his Crollian experiments with doubled efforts. One morning, he awoke with the idea of having them re-enact history, and he let out a laugh. He would persuade Napoleon, the one with the dicky tummy, to gather his army and attack the wardens, the 'fake nurses' in the blue overalls. He pestered him about it for days, trying to persuade him he was on Saint

Helena on the verge of his final escape, for this time the victory would be complete and clear cut.

Slowly it seemed Napoleon had understood what he wanted. But then brushed him off. The next day again the doctor reached a point where Napoleon asked about the inevitable resistance, the nurses' numbers, weighed up who he could count on and which arms were at his disposal, and even determined that the first move should be made on Tuesday when Polyáki was at the town committee. Tuesday came and nothing. Losing his patience, Doc Haris took him to task, what's going on, why be such a coward, be so submissive, it wasn't befitting of his name. At which Napoleon, a tailor driven insane by sewing buttonholes, turned to him and sonorously screamed in his face: 'But don't you know I'm mad!?'

It echoed around the yard. Then silence. Not so much from the content of what he said but how he'd said it. Napoleon's voice had cracked in the middle, creaked like a circus canvas, and, indeed, out through the flaps of the circus tent poured the laughing, thronging acrobats, the cymbal-wielding clowns, the whinnying horses. The whole enslaved troupe had broken free.

'I'm mad,' repeated a nearby, bracken-haired woman, and then the rest parroted it, nodding their heads. Doing their best to evoke from their throats that earlier sound, the outburst packed to the rafters with cheerful titters. They shouted in each other's ears. 'I'm mad!' The centuries-old building had never heard such words. I'm mad, I'm mad.

Liberated, high spirits rippled across the yard, with such potency even the hydrangeas shook and plaster dust trickled from their pink heads. Even the frailest who couldn't jump up from the bench clapped their hands or cackled, dribbling at the mouth. It was like they had set off towards something previously inaccessible because it was forbidden, or because they hadn't known the way.

Doc Haris was shocked. He was struck by how right he had been and how wrong he had been. It wasn't completely clear to him, but he still suspected that a mad person represented many in their fight for self-liberation. The lockdown, introduced in the name of reason, had ended and people had set off in search of the truth that lay dormant beneath the ruins of reason.

Napoleon quietly withdrew, and his hand, which had been prodding Doc Haris, returned to his paunch. But as if he had just spat out bitter food, he looked on the world with pleasure, contentment, relief. He made off on his usual route and the gravel merrily crunched beneath his slippers. A lasting, pleasant atmosphere settled in the yard, and beyond, in the corridors, and in the rage rooms where nobody was raging because Doc Polyáki was away at the Ayurvedic practitioners' conference, where he was elected chief secretary and had been invited on a month-long inaugural tour. Nobody got mired in quarrelling, in the muddy pool of daily bickering, from whose depths they constantly sought out the solid ground of understanding. Nobody desired to be anywhere else, they simply took pleasure in existing, blended into something whose meaning was unambiguous and something of course meaningless. In being part of the *unambiguous meaninglessness*.

Doc Haris grew lightheaded, he had been caught by the harsh late-morning sun. He was the one to kick off this miracle, the one to plant the twinkle in their eyes. Somehow reluctant now to play the philosopher in his loft space he stayed in the yard. It was nice to be in the sober world among its glorified martyrs, while Miklós vainly waited for him in the tea's dispersing steam. Adopting Haris's role, Miklós leant on his elbows in the window, watching the goings-on below. Suddenly he saw Dr Haris dashing after Napoleon, catching him, spinning him around with broad swings of the arms, and dancing, waltzing with him, then all of a sudden throwing off his shirt, and naked from the waist up, climbing the linden tree, hunkering down between the first branches as though in a nest, and declaring to the world: 'Dr Nietzsche is among you!'

Doc Haris had gone mad, and the nurses let him be, these things happened. Not to the nurses, but certainly to the doctors. They catch tuberculosis in lung hospitals. He was given three days. On the third day, Doc Haris was still wailing in the tree. He'd discovered that the world held much more truth than he'd previously seen in it, ordering himself to stop made no sense. He was given a week.

And then the nurses caught the sun too. Mind you, they used the opportunity to their tastes. They withdrew to their dens, gobbled down platefuls, drank, played cards, only dashed out to use the toilet, then brought in a bucket instead and never came out again. Everyone was left in peace. For years a productive rot had spread throughout the hospital, but now at last the constituents of this sparkling swarm had breached the surface. This Eden wasn't a garden because a garden, even an English garden, is the product of reason; it was a marsh, filled with a variety of silts that came to life in the sun and the warmth. This fermenting marsh, at first imperceptibly, but now quite plainly, contained the forces that created the world. Here, earthly existence lost its shamefully homogeneous history and crossed over to where such diversity reigned that reason, had it remained, would have trembled at the sight.

Miklós trembled. He didn't dare leave the loft. He watched the events below in horror. The folding screen had disappeared before his eyes. Insanity is sobering.

The residents of the house were gathering around the tree; without using words, but calling inarticulately, rhythmically flailing and frolicking, they summoned the whole yard, so that together, with the movements of a totemic ritual they could show their shared sensation of the force capable of wrenching them beyond their beings' real limitations. Rhythm is a strange thing, it can give boundless strength, which this time seemed powerful enough for them to survive without eating.

Hunger didn't sober them. What's more, it inebriated them to the point where they could endure without food. Oddly, Miklós didn't eat either and yet didn't feel hungry. Like in times of calamity or cataclysm, for seven days not a drop of water passed their lips.

On the seventh day, a terrible heatwave swept through the town, and above the yard the air sighed and throbbed. Miklós couldn't see well, he supposed his problems with his sight were back, frightened, he had stopped following what was happening below. Yet a visitor had arrived under the tree. A young woman, the very same that had visited Doc Haris a few weeks ago, was standing under the tree, reaching up into the air, and saying something, then with pleading gestures she pointed towards the exit, ever more desperately. Her arrival unsettled the congregation around the tree who surrounded her, sniffing her face and hair. From the hubbub, Miklós realized something was going on in the yard, he heard the girl's floods of tears, he heard as between sobs she called out a Christian name, evidently Doc Haris's. Miklós turned to the window. From the weeping, the girl took a turn for the worse, she began to heave, dropped to her knees, and fell to one side, twitching. Right away the old instinct took over and they started kicking her . . . Miklós knew it wasn't the girl they were kicking but the fit as they tried to drive it back into her, lest it take hold of them too. He also knew he ought to hurry down, he had to do something. The girl came around but jerked from the kicks and the blows. They shove and roll her towards the stone trough to smash her head to bits. The insanity has taken a form and found a goal. Where's Bumbi? Why isn't he jumping in? Why isn't he saving her? That's his job!? But Bumbi just stands there, seemingly resolute that he won't intervene. The girl's head is an inch from the rim of the trough. Perhaps the life has already left her. But no! She curls a protective arm around her head and the other she reaches out to stop her attackers. Who stop, panting. Yet on the other side of the stone trough, Uncle Lizard appears, holding a two-meter-long plank. He lifts it, high above his head, and steps out from behind the trough to bring it down, when with a deafening howl Doc Haris crashes from the tree and appears beside them with a single leap. Everyone freezes. Doc Haris bends over the girl, so tenderly that Miklós is ashamed because he's never seen two people so exposed. Haris props the girl up and practically lifts her off the ground as he leads her towards the gate. Miklós is so shaken by this unexpected turn, or perhaps what preceded it, that he faints. And when he comes around, he can't decide whether he really saw what he saw, or whether merely his imagination brought Haris down from the tree. And insomuch as it was his imagination's doing, was it then a warning of the inevitable deluge of matter's impulses, or the contrary, a formulation of the triumph of human ingenuity over matter's impulses? In any case, the question directed his attention to the flow of time. And indeed, an hour later, it was clear to Miklós what had happened to Doc Haris.

Translated by Owen Good

THE CLOISTER OF SANCTUARY

to Emil Novák

1

The man lurking by the narrow crack in the window can't make out too much. Ordinary desire begins to develop in his throbbing temples. Irina hurriedly pulls off her clothes, slips into a pullover and jeans. Bosom heaving, she crams a few smaller items into a shoulder bag. She looks around again, and finally sets off. In the doorway, a robust woman appears, her characteristic headdress makes her look even more imposing. Agota! the girl cries out in fear. *Folime ci mirie, denoste tu . . . si ciari!*—she adds, her words unintelligible. She does not use incomprehensible speech to try to get out but shoves the figure barring her way. At which point, Sister Agota shrieks hysterically, blocks the doorjamb with her left leg, buttressing herself with the right. The girl trying to get out is shorter than her—weighing at least twenty kilograms less—so that no matter how hard she tries, she cannot force the woman aside. And help is already arriving from the nearby rooms: lashing arms thrust Irina back into the depths of the closet. There's nothing inside there; only a bed and a kind of chest; she collapses onto the former and begins to whimper in a terrifying voice. Sister Agota grabs a fistful of her hair, jerking the girl's head back, forcing her to look directly into her face. Irina falls silent. When she lets her go, she starts up again: she grabs the girl and she shuts up, then she lets her go; her whimpering starts up again. Irina functions predictably: with the girl's hair firmly in her clutch, Agota can easily roll her this way and that, as if she were a rag.

What are you blathering about? Sister Agota asks her. The auburn tint in the locks of mahogany-dark hair falling across her fingers could be evidence that she's been colouring her hair.

Where did you hide your clothes? asks Sister Marta, imperiously stressing the word *clothes*.

We should burn all of her junk, advises the third woman; she's known as Ankuca, but everyone always adds 'the Zealous' to her name. You can't chase out the devil with lamp paraffin.

Are you a boy? What are these trousers for? Sister Teodosia adds, leaving aside the role of inert supernumerary and beginning to undress Irina.

Agota holds Irina down tight, pressing her head against the chest, so that Teodora, with the aid of Sister Marta, can pull off the trousers. Sister Agota reaches under the pullover with rapid movements, clutching at Irina's hair with her other hand; now the pullover can be peeled off with ease. In the meantime, Ankuca searches for the nun's habit tossed down a moment ago. At last, she finds it underneath the bed.

Marta rolls up the jeans and pullover and holds them under her arm. Agota is the last to leave. She locks the door with a key scooped out of her pocket, then mentions to Marta that instead of burning the clothes, it would be much better to give them to Nae Miru's granddaughter, Borinka the mute.

2

Petre watches the bird with his head cocked to one side. He's been sitting on the banks of the stream since the morning, but he still hasn't caught anything. He merely sits and stares. Now he's watching the robin as it hops across the branches of the black elderberry bush; in the meantime, a fish bites at the hook and drags it below the bank, winding the line onto a tree root reaching into the water. Petre tugs the rod in anger, but carefully, so that the hook won't snap off. And he might have to crawl under the bank anyway. He lingers for a moment longer in the mild sunshine. No sweeter land than this. The heart of Moldovia, its golden navel! He was glad things had worked out this way; life with the elders in Prutfalva wouldn't have been as good. Sooner or later, he would have been ordained. Father Dimitrie had instructed him to grow his beard, but he could hardly even manage a downy fuzz. Father Dimitrie's own beard reached down to his navel, his hair hung down to the middle of his back; yet he wasn't that much older than Petre himself.

He thinks of his father. When he came home in the evenings, the sunlight penetrated through his dishevelled hair, strangely enlarging his head. His father was no lucky angler himself, more often than not returning with empty baskets. He wasn't good at anything; he just kept stealing from the collective farm, and if he got some money, soon drank it all away.

The night his mother left, he beat Irina savagely, as if it were all her fault. All three of them sobbed. After bedtime, he snuggled up next to his sister, her breasts already fragrant with the scent of milk even though they were only barely beginning to swell. When their father strung himself up, they starved for three days. His sister took him to her breasts then as well— anything to make him stop howling. And if that proved to be of no solace, she sat him down on her foot, stretched out and stiffened, and rocked him back and forth.

Suddenly the line untangles itself, and Petre lifts a fish, hand-sized, out of the water. He removes it from the hook, then the hook itself, wraps the remaining worm segments around the hook; maybe he'll pull something out of the water now: the fish start to bite, and he plucks them out one after the other.

Kovrig approaches, walking alongside the bushes; the figure who had been lurking behind the palm-sized window. He's carrying the pigswill out from the kitchen. There's a problem with your sister, she needs to be disciplined again, he calls out. The Father wants to talk with you.

Annoyed, Petre begins to gather up his things. Just now when they're starting to bite, he grumbles. He mutters to himself on the path as well. His sister can never stay still for a moment. That was why they had to run away from the orphanage, because she was suddenly seized with this get-me-out-of-here. He would teach her one day, and she would live to regret it!

3

Kovrig, sweep up the breadcrumbs! says Father Dimitrie, as Kovrig begins to bow and scrape all around the tables. The room resembles a cafeteria, a long shelf placed along one of the walls. Father Dimitrie sits down at one of the tables, in front of Petre.

Your sister wants to leave.

I'll talk to her.

Good, that's absolutely right. Tell her this isn't a hotel. This is a sacred place. A place of sanctuary. Sister Agota suspects that the demon Natra has cast a spell on her. She's constantly screaming 'demosi'.

She wants to get the money that's owed her.

Fine, then, you go with her, Agota too. Uncle Misa can take you. But go now, and quiet her down, so she's not shouting all the time. Shove her down the well, lock her up in the cellar, just do something with her!

Petre sets off, but then comes to a dead halt in the doorway and turns around. But he doesn't say anything. He waits for Kovrig to catch up to him, and together they walk to the nuns' quarters.

Sister Agota arrives, spreads out her arms. You can't go now, she's been possessed by Natra. Marta is giving her an exorcism, she knows what to do. Come back tomorrow, everything will be fine by then.

They go to the left, back to the valley, back to the pigsties. From afar, they hear the piglets' hungry squealing.

Kovrig's tongue is loosened, although he isn't as a rule loquacious. Maybe she's really been possessed by the devil. Once I heard the neighbour woman screaming, you couldn't make out a word. Father Seraphim came and exorcised her with rooster's blood; then the devil took possession of our pig. It began to speak the language of humans. The entire village came to witness the miracle, but Father Seraphim ran a dagger through its throat, drained the blood onto the ground, and then built a fire right in that very place. so that Satan couldn't escape. Everyone was craving the fresh blood.

Petre says now what he wished he could have said to the priest. When we arrived in Pelevin, we spoke that language together. We made up words. *Denoste* means money owed, a debt.

4

The case of Irina comes up while the Father is meeting with the lawyer in the resplendent garden.

Domu Avramescu, there are more and more such cases. Last Sunday, there were three of them from the city. Rolling around in convulsions before the iconostasis, rattling sounds coming from their throats. I had to ask my younger brother to come help me.

I have faith in you, my son—that is, my Father.

I cannot be victorious alone.

I'll have a little chat with the bishopric, they'll arrange for your brother to have his ordination.

Not that! Archimandrite Bladiu is the devil himself. Lately, he was seen flying in his chair above the village.

The bishops require a cautious touch, I warned you about that last time. I'll help you out as much as I can. Because I know that what I give to you, I also give to Christ. And I'll get it all back in the world beyond.

The two men sit next to each other in swaying hammock chairs, the Father lurching back and forth a little uncertainly. A child with long black hair sits before them in the grass, looking at some pictures. His face displays unaccustomed agitation.

Your descendants will be so proud of you, Domu Avramescu, says the Father as he bends down and caresses the boy's head. Has anyone told you how much your little boy looks like you?

Domu Avramescu used to be delighted when people took his grandson to be his son. But ever since he returned from his pilgrimage to Mount Athos, he finds the child's presence vexing. And he has a headache to boot. Tumbling round and round in the crystal goblet on the table behind him, a painkiller tablet fizzles: the fragments tear away from each other, race wildly in the water, disappear without a trace.

Since his recent return from the Sacred Mount, the lawyer has allowed his beard to grow, and a golden cross now dangles from around his neck. Not a single grey hair is visible in his beard; his eyes are the same deep black, his face rosy-cheeked, and the cross is 24-carat Turkish gold. He makes money not only by lawyering but through his ownership of the local grocery-store chain, the three largest eateries (where you can enjoy the very best roast pork in all of Moldavia) and of course the textile factory as well, though it's true that on paper his wife is listed as the owner. His wife Lenuca herself started out as a textile worker; even today everyone in the factory knows and likes her. Of course, among the factory workers, there are those who don't much appreciate being obligated to pledge a part of their salary to the patronage of the monastery.

We must return to the old faith, Little Father!

Dr Avramescu's harsh, coarse voice contrasts strongly with his dreamy gaze. His garden, too, is a study in contradictions: in the front are flower beds and rose arbours; in the back, blood-spattered tables and drunken pig slaughterers unsteadily hacking away at dead swine. Pieces of liver, kidney and lung sizzle away in lard on the smouldering iron stove, for all to partake. The lawyer first offers some to the child who, making a face, turns his head away. Father Dimitrie, however, is glad to have a bite. To one side is a round table, laid with a white cloth and opulently gleaming fruits; slices of cantaloupe arranged in a circle around watermelons sliced in half, forming a captivating sun-disk in the middle of the table. The lawyer has all his fresh fruits brought in from Greece. He announces this fact to the patriarch, moreover strongly intimating yet again that he will send the Father himself to the Sacred Mount, to the elders of the Greek Church. I'll make a bishop of you, then we'll see how you talk! He gets up from the hammock, steps over to the table, downs the half-dissolved painkiller in one gulp, slices off a piece of seedless melon and, impaling it on the end of his knife, tries to slide it into the child's mouth. Mechanically, the child turns away, but then reaches back for the fruit, grabbing at it with his fingers and stabbing himself on the knife's point. He cries out in pain, holding his hand up, scarlet blood spurting forth. Artemie, the house servant, comes running, bringing a scrap of cobweb scavenged from somewhere. This will stop it! she pants.

5

The lawyer is having a chat in the park of the main square, sitting on a cast-iron bench. Next to him is a stout man with curly hair, who keeps removing and replacing his glasses. Everyone calls him 'the Writer', although he isn't strictly one, merely the editor of the local paper—although he did pen two works on the monasteries of Moldavia. He speaks in a transfigured voice, nearly chanting the words. From time to time, they lower their voices; another person is sitting at the other end of the bench.

Domu Avramescu, we must return to our old beliefs. I myself have reinstated the old calendar. Why, the bishops have put up their own church for sale. Just take a look at their faces—not one man among them is a real priest.

You be quiet: with a mug like yours, you could, at the very best, serve as a harem guard.

Mariora says I look just like Tomica, the cupbearer of Voivode Ştefan in the paintings of Luchian. We are, in fact, distant relations. It was Tomica's lash that drove out the despotic Voivode, foreingn usurper of the throne. We have always only wanted what's good for the country. My father was a member of the Royal Privy Council; he died in one of Gheorghe Gheorghiu-Dej's prisons.

Communism too was brought to us by foreigners. Because that is what we Moldavians are like: our gates are open to everyone. And they never come one by one, but in hordes greater than cities.

I say, it wouldn't hurt us to be more suspicious. We can't even tell when danger is staring us full in the face. Like when the gaze of the frog fixes itself on the gun barrel and cannot perceive the baleful outline of the steamroller moving towards it. Where God is adored, there must be evil as well. Now, the threat to us comes from Rome . . .

I know that Bladiu is one of the Pope's men, but let him think we don't know. We must await the right time . . .

Have you spoken with the Brethren?

Not so loud! Yes, we are in communication with each other every day, thanks to the fruit transporters. Their counsel is to be very cautious: Bladiu has Russian connections; you can't really make out his game.

If he ends up being named patriarch, there's nothing we can do about it.

We can't allow his appointment! We must discredit him in time.

We succeeded in making Archimandrite Carpina withdraw . . .

The archimandrite stepped aside of his own accord, my friend! So he could work in peace and quiet . . .

Domu Avramescu, if you didn't exist, we would have to invent you!

Our people have never been harlots. There were those who walked the path of whoredom, but the common folk never did. They never spread their legs, nor did they violate others. Why? Because they were wily. I have always considered wiliness to be one of my trades, and I know a thing or two, 'why the fly croaks'. Well, would you like to join me this weekend at the cloister?

I don't think that Mariora would take kindly to that.

Your problem is that you take her too seriously. I'll give you some money, just get yourself some girls.

That's all I need! She gave me a crack on the nose with the telephone just today, as you can see yourself.

I hadn't noticed. But come to think of it, yesterday your nose did look smaller.

She said I wrote lies about her. Yet everything happened exactly as I described it.

Can I give you some good advice? For people to be happy, you must lie to them. Hoodwink them, and they'll trust you. Kick their guts in, and they'll throw themselves at your feet.

I'm afraid you're right there.

You tell my life story the way it is, though. No need to lie. I built up the monastery, and I'll build a few more as well. They will all be consecrated by the bishop. Because he's selling himself not only to the Antichrist but to me as well.

You have done so much for the nation, Domu Avramescu. Dimitrie and the others would have long since starved to death. The Pelevin orphanage justly bears your name.

The young man sitting at the other end of the bench, who had until now been tensely eavesdropping on the conversation, suddenly jumps up, pirouettes around and, kneeling before the lawyer, takes his hand. Do I have the honour of speaking to Doctor Avramescu, benefactor of the monastery, saviour of the church . . . I am Dimitrie's brother, I've just arrived by train and I'm going to see him right now. I too am a theologian. My brother spoke very highly of you, may the blessings of God be upon you!

6

Father Dimitrie pulls his black mitre all the way down to his eyebrows. His stature is close to the ground, his movements nimble, all his strength in his shoulders, like a bull. He can feel a watchful gaze on himself even when coming from behind. Despite his bulk, he played goalkeeper for the orphanage football team; his saves were so impressive that people flocked from all around to watch him play. Hardly would the forward position his leg for the kick when Father Dimitrie had already thrown himself into precisely the right corner. And there is yet one further rare skill that he has been granted: with one glare, he can subdue all the troublemakers in the stands. Already, his younger brother worships him as a saint, so affected that he can hardly speak. He kneels before him, kisses his hand. Father Dimitrie allows this, and only then has him rise. His younger brother stands at least a head taller than he, but this is of no significance.

On the train as well, the people had spoken of all the miracles that he had enacted in the past weeks. A lady from the capital city had been suffering from migraines for three years; the Father cured it by spitting on the crown of her head. He spoke to a child who was causing disturbances during the church service, and the very next day the child was performing multiplication and division even though he had never been to school. A university student sought his intervention during

157

exam week; Father Dimitrie didn't even reply but simply nodded, and the very next day the student scored the highest marks of the entire University of Iaşi, even though he hadn't cracked a book open during the entire semester.

Among the passengers, there were also those whispering in the devil's own tongue. It wasn't Father Dimitrie that they were aiming to harm, but the lawyer. There were those who—leaning down to the younger brother's ear to speak over the rattling of the train—passed on the rumour that the lawyer had reestablished the collective farm; he kept pigs, two hundred of them at the very least, but he has cows too, and provides the city marketplaces with vegetables. The entire monastery is working for him; it rounds up the novices and nuns from the local orphanage. Nae Misu, the director of the collective farm, was also the director of the orphanage. In addition to that, you just have to ask yourself: what kind of a monastery is it where men and women are doing the Lord's work together . . .

Nae Misu was in fact the administrator of the Pelevin orphanage. He'd picked up a little of every trade and could even be called upon to recite the liturgy. When Irina, in spite of everything, was taken to the hospital, it was because Sister Marta, who'd been entrusted by the Father with her care, had worked, before taking the veil, in the ward of Dr Parvalescu, an ungodly, ill-bred man who treated all women like scullions, swore like a trooper, beat the patients so hard that none of them were ever cured—and he wouldn't so much as give you the time of day until you slipped an envelope stuffed with banknotes into his pocket. Marta would have liked to tell him right to his face that he would only make the girl's condition worse . . . All the same, the ambulance was called, but the ambulance never arrived; for one thing, there were no available vehicles, and for another, any car sank up to its axles in the mud on the dirt road leading up to the monastery, whether coming or going, not even to mention that washing off the mud from the undercarriage was the ambulance driver's duty; in the end Nae Misu took the girl in the monastery's, that is to say Domu Avramescu's Dacia, so that Dr Parvalescu could have a look at her and in no way whatsoever discover what the problem was. As expected, he did say something, but he couldn't cure her; two weeks went by, or more exactly fifteen days, and then he sent for Marta to come take her away, she's fine now—although the two of them knew full well that nothing had changed; she had only been pumped so full of tranquillizers that she could hardly get up on her feet to walk.

Dr Parvalescu was, of course, exceedingly irritated by Marta's self-satisfied expression—he could have strangled her! He could hardly wait for her to leave, then took refuge in a rabid frenzy. The patients, strapped into their caged beds, awaited their injections, but he didn't care; he tore his stethoscope from his neck and flailed away at the rusty iron of the clattering bed cages, kicking hard at the bed frames, foaming at the mouth and cursing in rage, howling out vilifications against Marta's bottomless womb—it had tried to devour him, but he would cure her, he'd smash her like a hammer. All the while, he felt just as small and helpless as the figure in the white medical coat writhing convulsively in the pupils of the patients' eyes, as they jerked back and forth in terror.

7

So now Marta's time has come. *Doamne milujeste*!

She awakens at dawn on Sunday morning. The sky outside is stirring; the same feeling as when the sleeper next to us rolls over on one side. A large body. At least as large as Agota's. Although if the sky rolls over to one side, that cannot be compared to anything else.

She gets up, already knowing what she has to do: the demon must be cast out with frogs' blood, not just that of any frog, but one that got drunk on Saint Vasilij's Day, that is to say the first day of the New Year. Because on that day, when the church bells toll at noon, the waters of the countryside turn to wine! Concoctions of various kinds sit in readiness on the shelves of Marta's cabinet. Everyone knows about her collecting excursions; one of the sisters always accompanies her. At first, Nae Misu helped her with unearthing the frogs on Saint Vasilij's Day, though lately she's been taking Kovrig along: he grumbles less and doesn't get quite as drunk on the last evening of the old year. Extracting the blood from a trepanned frog is truly one of the secret arts. Now, she takes from the vessel the tiniest dose, carries it to the girl and smears it on her forehead. In two days, an additional dose will be necessary, this time dribbled around her mouth, but even that isn't enough. It seems now that it isn't Natra that has possessed her, but something else. She speaks to Father Dimitrie, tells him that never before has she met with such deep-rooted depravity. The people of the village will help, nods the Father in agreement. He's proud of how, in a scant few months, he has been able to forge a true *comunitate* from the village folk.

Recently, he cured the forester's daughter, after she'd lan-guished in a Bucharest hospital for weeks. The forester sent him three winters' worth of firewood in gratitude; there it stood, split and stacked in the woodshed. The power of prayer is the power of the saints, my brethren; the pill and the powder are the contrivances of Man, that is to say the Devil himself!

While Holy Mass is being served, Marta and Nae Misu place Irina outside in front of the church, so that the congre-gation as it comes swarming out can utter a prayer above her, and the many prayers will thicken together like well-kneaded dough. Irina lies prostrate on the grass, tied to a hastily impro-vised cross: two boards stacked on top of each other; the twine holding her ankles and wrists stretched tight enough to pluck out a note. A long queue snakes out of the church entrance. The people standing one after the other mutter a prayer and then spit onto the girl; that is, on the Devil. For the Devil is such that he has no body; he merely wanders on this earth, taking possession of human beings. Most important of all is to cast holy water upon him, and if there is no holy water to be found, then we can use our own spittle, for saliva, in the end, comes from our bodies and our bodies are nothing but the handiwork of God Himself. Also, the urine of the saints has its own healing powers. There are many such cases, although in general the Books of Molitvenic are silent on this issue.

After spitting, it is necessary to utter a curse, because in this way, the Devil evaporates like water.

—May the sun shrivel your womb!

—And your bowels be gnawed by spiders!

—And snakes crawl through your innards!

—And frogs befoul your eyes!

Even the children come up with curses. One of them, from among the (purportedly illegitimate) children of one of the lawyer's favourite shepherds, suddenly stands still—nothing is coming to mind. He remains paralysed until someone next to him jostles him forward. Immediately, he runs back, wriggling his way back into the line, and cries out towards the figure laid down on the grass: may the devil bang you with his scabrous cock! At this, the line surges forward, as if a dam has burst: no verbose embellishments now, they just spit, hurling a few coarse words as they do so, and move on. Soon, none of them is left.

Only one woman doesn't spit. She waits at the corner of the church. Deeply troubled, she watches the procession, waiting to speak with someone from the congregation. But, taking a shortcut through the sacristy and the atrium, they have already disappeared into the church with its shining tin-plate roof.

8

Foli . . . tudo . . . rabojni . . . Irina suspects that the nuns standing around her don't understand what she's saying, but her words aren't meant for them. If they had tied her up and beat her with wet rags, they weren't going to help her now. She is hoping that Petre will hear and come set her free at last. Every part of her body is burning, as if living flesh were touching the fibrous boards.

Petre! The cry bursts out of her when the closet door opens, and someone is standing there in the crack of the door opening. It's not her younger brother, however, but the Father, who stands waiting, arms crossed amid the light radiating from behind him, as if fully aware of the effect produced by the illumination swirling in the background. He stands mute, while the sisters, flabbergasted at the miracle, drop to their knees. Then he shouts out to them, his voice forced out from somewhere inside his throat: subdue her, silence the wretch somehow, the entire monastery is ringing with her howls. Sister Agota shoves a towel, twisted like a bridle, into Irina's mouth, and then with Marta's help stretches the two ends across the wooden plank, tying them together.

That, however, proves to be of no help at all. The girl continues to whimper; it's as if the voice weren't even coming from her mouth. The effect is terrifying. Petrified, the nuns turn to the figure standing in the door, as if wishing, through their own muteness, to transmit some matter of ultimate significance.

Father Dimitrie moves closer, exasperated. Go out, I don't want you to have any troubles! He clutches the enormous cross dangling on his chest and holding it in front of himself, bends over Irina. The nuns scurry out of the closet. Now the priest remains alone with the girl who, as if sensing his approach, falls silent.

Silent, with open eyes. More precisely, her eyes were open before, but now they are filled with watchfulness. The tiny light-spheres of attention begin to move in a straight line towards the light-sphere of the golden cross, dissolving into it. This enlarged sphere of illumination is peopled by minute human figures, smiling, hastening forms. Their faces are minuscule, yet their slightest trembling is distinctly visible. Just as visible is the joy that pervades them when Irina comes into their midst. She is in jeans, a fashionably styled leather bag on her shoulder with the cheerful green inscription *Es geht gut* . . . I'm overjoyed to see you, says the most luminous microscopic figure, extending a hand. Overjoyed? asks Irina. Yes, and I would like you to stay. Irina's happiness blazes up like a flame, the sudden shower of sparks sweeping everyone away from her side, and only she can be seen now kneeling before the icon, which does not bear the image of the Redeemer, but that of Father Dimitrie . . . He truly loves you, someone whispers from between hands clasped in prayer. And I love you too! A burst of blazing sweetness, and the scene breaks apart; now the courtyard in the Pelevin orphanage is visible, the corner ramshackle building, and at its base stands Dimitrie, still a beardless teenager; he smiles at Irina and says: Irina, my betrothed! Both of them can be recognized from their smiles.

Suddenly, it's as if outside in the atrium, darkness has fallen: once more the lurking figure becomes visible in the hand-sized window. And perhaps it has somehow become caught there, because the figure does not move even though the sight within should make it want to flee.

9

Irina no longer screams. If her bonds are undone, she no longer kicks; if someone sits her up she remains sitting up; if she is helped to her feet she keeps standing; if given a gentle push she starts walking. She no longer soils her little chamber as she did before. Marta, in raptures, conveys the news to Father Dimitrie. Irina is sad, that's the only problem, otherwise she's quite well. The heavenly guest has healed her. In time, we might start giving her some chores to do.

First go for the money, the cleric nods.

10

They are sitting in the car, the same butter-yellow Dacia, and Petre is with them as well now. Nervous faces, perspiring bodies in black habits pressed against each other; four people occupy the rear seat. They drive along the winding roads, Petre giving the directions. He knows the region well: for three years they lived in the city, Irina minded the children while he worked on nearby farms.

We've come for the money, the youth says to the family gathered on the arched veranda of the house.

It isn't your money, but Irina's.

She's here as well, sitting in the car.

So why doesn't she get out?

Petre looks towards the car. The nuns begin to climb out, Irina peeled away from their bodies like plaster off a wall, confusion on her face. Her eyes can hardly be seen; she pulls her kerchief over her face.

Come inside, says Mrs Prikop in confusion.

From the outside, the house looks completely different from the other Moldavian houses, but inside it is exactly the same: a cosy nest lined with carpets. Devotional images hang on the walls. Two of the nuns, Marta and Ankuca, cross themselves.

Kovrig stays outside in the car, but then he too gets out, gazing across the fence into the house until he strikes up a conversation with the Prikops' neighbour. Petre, looking out from the veranda entrance, can see they're laughing about something.

So you've come for the money?

Irina nods. In the meantime, the Prikops' youngest child, three-year-old Paula, runs in carrying a bright polka-dotted ball. Smiling, she holds it out to Irina, but the girl doesn't reach for it. Why don't you play with her? Mrs Prikop asks. I haven't been given permission to touch the ball, comes the answer.

Mr Prikop, at these words, sniggers audibly. His wife looks at him, annoyed.

Well, the money isn't here. We put it in the bank.

So go and take it out, says Marta.

All right, then. The only thing is, we've put it into a fixed deposit account, says Mrs Prikop's daughter-in-law.

But you can still take it out, couldn't you?

Of course we can, but that would be stupid. And why does Irina need the money right now? She said she wanted to buy a house near here. She was saving up for it and going back to Germany to earn the rest. Mrs Adamik already told her she could go, her old employers were waiting for her, and this time she didn't even need a visa.

Do you want to go? Marta asks Irina.

The girl does not reply.

Do you want to go?

The girl gestures, indicating she does not.

This isn't Irina! You're trying to cheat her! Mrs Prikop cries out.

At this—to everyone's surprise—old Grandfather Prikop creeps out of the cupboard, a tin box in his hand. He opens the box: in it is the money. The old man is so little that hardly anyone notices him. Only when he has already handed the bundle of notes to Irina do the rest of the Prikops seem to come to life. They swoop down on her, but it is too late. As if having finished a good day's work, the old grandfather crawls up onto the glazed-tile stove and huddles there. He looks at no one, but simply blinks like an owl.

Irina is blinking in just the same way as they travel back in the car. A black Mercedes with oval headlights comes into view: for an instant, the fleeting image is frozen in the pupils of her eyes. The person travelling in the Mercedes quickly looks away, as if jarred by the sight, by the gaze that surprisingly became interwoven with his own.

Irina's stare clings to the gleaming coachwork of the Mercedes, and travels with it for hours, racing along with it well after darkness has fallen along German autobahns, through the neon-bathed streets of German cities, until it arrives at a country house beside a lake. In the distance, in the crimson light of the setting sun on the lake's flickering surface, are the shadows of sails like gargantuan fish in a sea of illumination.

11

In the courtyard of the monastery, a yellow-legged black hen scuttles to and fro. Its head has just been cut off, or more precisely, still hangs from the neck by a single slender thread of skin. Blood gushes forth in streams, the hen-body runs in ever faster circles of ever-smaller radii and collapses; now the legs only scratch at the sky a few last times. Irina can see it all, but she has no desire to be a part of this particular spectacle. She is doubled over, like the old grandfather. To assume residence in one's own body, all the way into its depths, down into the void, deep beneath the earth's surface, to crawl down through the hole of a molehill, creep forever and then nest inside this burrow, in this characteristic pose. To grow a cocoon like a caterpillar. To fill up one's lacunae with lacunae. To lie prostrate like that.

As she steps towards Irina, Ankuca sees that she has once again been possessed by the devil. She is jabbering again in that incomprehensible tongue. Words sputter out of her. Ghastly! Ankuca grabs her own ears, even covering them with her palms, as she runs to fetch Marta.

Right at that moment, Marta is furious at Kovrig, because he didn't leave the vegetable cart where she told him to. She's furious at Elena, who sleeps next to Irina: she's not supposed to leave her alone and she just heard from Ankuca that she's done precisely that. And she's furious at Ankuca for bringing bad news.

12

Irina doesn't want to get up. The cords are tightened around her body, her legs forced straight, they won't leave her alone. First they straighten her arms, kneeling on top of her, binding her, like a pig during slaughter—the same thick cord. And she squeals like a pig. Then suddenly, she lies prostrate, her body so empty, like a worn-out shoe kicked off by a foot. She falls mute. Even silence can be maddening. Sister Teodora clutches at her ears. Agota and Marta search all over Irina's body, until they hit upon the point where the evil went into her, where it hurts the most, and her screams are so loud that the wooden planks start to tremble.

13

The screaming passes over the entire village, even though it lies quite a distance from the monastery. The animals fall silent. The shrieking goes wandering among the gently sloping hillsides. Above the monastery is an oddly shaped cloud; the villagers look up at it and cross themselves several times over.

14

Now the lawyer is in his sumptuous quarters; in the semi-darkness, bodies lie languorously. All around him are beautiful young girls. He tries his best to arouse desire in them. Next to the lawyer's decrepit body, the beautiful forms become hideous. My darling, you little bumpkin, you shagger!

Don't speak! the lawyer shouts, don't disturb me . . . Even the windows begin to tremble. On the lawyer's body, there is only the golden double-barred cross; he raises it between his fingers and begins to pray. Oh Lord, grant me the power to resist temptation! Oh Lord, give me the strength to conquer evil!

15

The time for vespers has come; limping Marta begins to beat the bell; Marta the healer and the other three head towards Irina in the closet behind the porch. Last evening, they discovered that it was more comfortable for them to rest one end of the wooden plank onto the porch which also forms the support for the closet wall; this way they don't have to stand in the draught, and if her feet are placed higher than her head, the girl can't scream as much.

Marta is now trying with devils' ashes; Agota reads aloud from the Books of Molitvenic, Teodora sprinkles holy water from a gold-rimmed demitasse cup with a teaspoon.

This morning I saw, as I opened the door, a mouse and a snake running out from underneath her clothes.

The herb tansy is a good pesticide against mice . . .

My neighbour in the village, old Miron's wife, used garlic for everything. Even when her sister-in-law, out of revenge, tried to get the cow's milk to dry up.

If you want milk to spoil by the next day, let a drop of verbena tincture fall into the empty canister. But you can cancel the curse by letting fall one drop of wax from a consecrated candle into the milk.

If a child drinks from this milk, it will fall deadly ill.

Never allow a child to step in front of a mirror before its teeth start to come in, because the child will become mute. Or it will start raving like this one here. In that case, you must smash the mirror, and have them walk barefoot across the shards . . .

This one can't even walk! We'd get nothing for making her try.

Whoever eats of many fish shall also fall mute. However, he who is born in the month of the fishes will never turn mute.

At times my niece says something you can hardly understand. She's a clever girl, though, she speaks French, English and even German, but little good it does her, she doesn't like to talk much.

Her father was a fisherman; it's no surprise she turned out that way. The guardian from the orphanage was here recently. Said her father strung himself up. And she was swinging on him.

Her mind always ran to perversity.

You can't give water to children while they're still suckling at the breast. That also makes them insane.

The best thing would be to keep her from drinking anything for a few days. Let us not slake the thirst of the Devil with holy water. If he goes out of her, then she'll get some.

We should thrash her with nettles.

Nettles work against the demon Natra, but this one is possessed by something else. We need the icon covering . . . Twist it three times, tie nine knots in it while reciting the verse to it. Then you dampen it, but first place a lump of coal in the water, and a black thread. The fire burns away the bad, the water purifies the good. Tie the wart with the thread from the water.

They tell a story of how recently Fanika, using a sanctified handkerchief, drove away vagabonds who cast the evil eye on the village.

That crazy Fanika, she's always mixing things up. She cast off Anna's seed, but she made that girl's blood flow, and it's been flowing ever since.

The best remedy for bleeding is to sit in coal dust.

I've told Anna a thousand times: she should come to us, we'll take care of her, she'll have everything she needs. But no, she lives in her own little world. The Lord doesn't thrash with a cane.

16

It is a particular thing that the bodies of those consecrated to sanctity should be so full of the thorns of life. Although the sisters are adroit in discovering a solution. They say that when the lunar month of a new arrival has aligned with the others, only then can she be consecrated, because now she has entered the community with body and soul. During this time— reminding them in so many ways of the life they have abandoned—the sisters pray more than usual. There is less time for Irina. Marta, in particular, is much in demand after Dr Avramescu's daughter asked her to do something about the ants infesting her house; Marta found a potion that worked with devastating effect. Ever since then, everyone is calling her. She sprinkles fruit brandy on the threshold, and from that point on no ant ever crosses it again. Of course, it's hardly any ordinary spirits that she uses, but one distilled by the Devil, as she says. Of course it isn't distilled by Satan, but rather that *atropa belladonna*, or deadly nightshade, is soaked in the potion.

When she gets home from her tiring day, she goes in to see Irina to sprinkle some brandy on her as well (and it's good she remembered to do this). The girl's eyes are as wide open as a great burdock leaf; they shine frighteningly. So frighteningly that Marta yells for Sister Agota to come, and Agota calls out to Ankuca.

Bind up her eyes, says Sister Agota, trembling. Ankuca throws a rag on the girl's face, then she tightens the cords on the girl's wrists and ankles. She winds a chain around the entire body, because they've run out of cord: with the chain she encircles the body at least ten times. Their palms are reddened from the rusty chain, they wipe their hands off on their robes.

After they are done, Sister Agota, as she leaves, pulls the cloth from Irina's face. Those eyes as wide as great burdock leaves are like two dark bottomless pits. Sister Agota clutches at the wooden-plank wall, fearful she might collapse. She turns her head away and gropes her way out. She bolts the door shut. Then the body begins to twitch, convulsing like the limbs of a Daddy Long Legs. Someone who had been watching through the window falls away from there, as if having fainted; a dull thumping sound is heard.

17

Petre once again stands before Father Dimitrie. The Father is demanding he account for a stolen pig. He also mentions that his sister is behaving in an ever more disturbing fashion. They can't chase the devil out of her. Although he had already thought that everything would be fine. He himself will have to try again to treat her, but he is so exhausted, so much work has he.

Are you engaging in acts of fornication? he asks Petre.

No, never.

Have you both committed a sin?

No, never.

What are you hiding?

Nothing . . .

You are not telling me the truth, the Father says, leaping up, and rolling his eyes, he stares fixedly at the boy.

Petre breaks, he begins to wail:

Yes, I confess, my Father, I understand what she says to me, because she taught me that speech. When we were little she spoke that way to me. We went to find my mother, but we didn't find her anywhere. We walked everywhere, I don't remember where we got money for the trip. Since then we have never spoken that way, but I understand what she's saying. She's saying that He will conquer the entire world— that the Antichrist will soon come, and He will devour the good as if it were a frog. That's what she is saying. She's asking me to free myself and go with her, but I will not go; I want to remain here with you.

You're babbling nonsense, the Father waved him away. Then he again looked up, rolling his eyes. I'll take care of you too, you're next!

18

The slender tower of the graveyard church seems as if it were built to resemble a human body; at the very least its colours evoke the illumination of rusty flesh. There are at least 500 people crowded there. They have come from all over, thanks in part to the newspaper reports. The characteristic outlines of the monastery are clearly visible even in the distance, with the inevitable cloud floating above. The cart arrives bearing the coffin, those standing close burst into sobs. Sobs and curses.

After the interment of the coffin, nobody moves; they take small, peculiar steps that lead them nowhere, standing around the grave. There is confusion in their eyes. Then someone begins, and others follow suit, as they begin to curse the residents of the distant monastery. They pronounce damnation upon the priest, the nuns, upon the faithless, each one outdoing the other in curses. Their emotions are unleashed in their words. They drift to one corner of the grave, and stand there; then, as if speaking to reporters, they turn to an invisible camera, and they say—with wide gestures, rooted to the spot—what they would do to the murderers. At first, they pronounce: They are all murderers!—then they describe how they would do finish them off. Irina's stepfather (her mother wasn't able to come, because she is paralysed like a tree stump, her stepfather only keeps her because he needs the welfare payments, otherwise he would have handed her over to the Old People's Home, might as well free up the bed), in brief, the stepfather is now yelling into the imaginary camera that he would strangle all of them all tied up together, he would roll them into the river, but no, let them suffer for a long time, instead he would toss them into the carrion ditch.

As twilight falls, the cemetery becomes empty. Only one woman remains next to the grave. She was waiting by the corner of the church to talk to the nuns or the father. She was the one who raised Irina in the orphanage. She wears a black silk scarf on her head, as if mourning a close relative. The sorrow on her face dissolves into beauty. She does not speak to an imaginary camera, instead she speaks to an imaginary interlocutor as she looks at the clumps of earth: Is it true, were you there next to her? She raises her head, and she glances into the eye of an angel, cut out from a tin sheet, on the neighbouring grave. You were with her till the end, weren't you?

19

Irina's death plays itself out again, as if the caretaker from the orphanage, Maria, were imagining it. Irina lies alone, the closet dark and damp around her. But standing next to her is an angel in white garments, more luminous than any white seen in this world; it is more like blue, the blue sky of a sunlit day. Now it's as if the closet was appearing through Irina's eyes: there are beetles everywhere. The angel transforms, and in its place there now hangs a bat, or more precisely, it zigzags back and forth, hunting the beetles. Then it plunges to the ground, and the sound of the cracking exoskeleton of an enormous beetle can be heard. In the meantime, it casts a dreamy glance, first at the empty window opening, then at the girl, in whose eyes the light has died out. The lake of the eyes has suddenly grown dark.

20

Again back to the cemetery. At the entrance, brandy and sweet plaited egg-bread await those departing. Both are the gift of the village priest who is performing the service. Once again, the curses are heard directed towards the faithless of the monastery, the priest approving each one.

21

During the burial, the bishopric delegation arrives; Teofil, the bishopric secretary, leads them. He demands the sacred anti-mension, without which it is impossible to complete a liturgy. It's on the orders of Bishop Badiu, please understand! The nuns line up in a living chain before the church entrance. Father Dimitrie walks behind them, entering the church, the secretary nods, thinking that their struggles had borne fruit nonetheless. The Father immediately hides the altar cloth, trimmed with lace, in his vest pocket, and from the moment he steps out, not a word is spoken. He reaches the cellar entrance, darting glances directed his way, then hurries in, bolting the door from the other side. The bishopric delegation, along with the gendarmes accompanying them, turn to stone in their stupefaction. Then a young, gangly caloyer reaches across the heads of the crowd and gives the bishop's secretary a good whack. Who was that? Teofil, the secretary, asks in shock. But he doesn't see, and no one knows. The scene repeats itself a few more times. The blows get bigger and bigger. He asks the sergeant and the gendarmes to intervene, but the gendarmes, who are just standing around getting in the way, don't see anyone, respectively they see the young priest, but they think he is a part of the delegation. They don't understand what the secretary wants, and confusedly slink off to their grey terrain vehicles.

The bishop's secretary sets off after them, while the lawyer explains to him how the girl died. She choked because she was tied up too tightly, she couldn't breathe properly. Even her mouth was stuffed. Her lungs became ever flatter, like a punctured football.

At the mention of football, the secretary pricks up his ears, remembering that the Germany–Brazil match is about to start on TV, but he doesn't say anything, who knows what kind of a person this lawyer is. If he gets a move on, he might even catch the beginning, there's nothing to do here anyway, and it would be better for them to leave before the crowd gets too angry.

One of the members of the delegation notes that Father Dimitrie was an excellent football player; he used to play on the university team, and they always gave those theologians from Bucharest a thorough thrashing. The Germany–Brazil match is about to start, says the lawyer, motioning to his driver to open the car door. Then, for the entire trip back, they talk only about football, weighing the chances of that evening's match.

22

The tall gangly priest who had dealt the blow to the secretary is blocking the road, when the red Dacia, packed with reporters, sets off from the village towards the monastery. The driver, leaning out the lowered window, asks if they're headed in the right direction. The priest doesn't answer, he doesn't even move. In the meantime people arrive from the village, someone cries out: There are the traitors! An incomprehensible word follows, but the others take up the cry, yelling. Corrupters of children!—one man points at the oldest of the journalists. He gazes around impotently, his colleagues looking at him with consternation. No one understands what's going on. More and more people are standing around the car, it's inconceivable, as if the people had climbed out from the bushes. The journalists try to secure the doors, but it's too late, they're wide open, enraged faces leaning over the faces of the journalists. A female reporter wants to call the police, but someone grabs her mobile phone, throws it onto the ground, and stamps on it, as if it were a bug.

23

Miss Maria from the orphanage is talking to the television crew. There's no point in them snooping around, they'll never be able to find out what really happened. Because the truth is what's left out of every story.

The television crew is crammed into the cutting room. Nodding, they listen to Maria. At the beginning of a new sequence of pictures, the enormous face of the Writer appears on the monitor. The female reporter asks him how much money he thinks the monastery is getting for home exorcisms. The Writer changes the subject, speaking of the roots of the ancient liturgy of the Eastern Orthodox Church. Nothing must ever change. The essence of our church is constancy. We must return to our ancient calendar. Change disturbs the people. We must do everything the same as when, in the act of consecration, we transmit the touch of the hand of God.

Is there such a thing as exorcism? the female reporter asks. Everything is fixed in certain rules, answers the Writer. We may not misunderstand things. The activities of the priests are sacramental, full of symbolism, let's not drag it into the mud. If we do not have enough faith or fortitude to understand the secret, then let us not tamper with it.

Suddenly a woman steps into the picture, and begins to hit the Writer on the head with her purse.

The Writer jumps up and runs away, the woman following right after him. The picture turns white.

24

Marta and Ankuca walk next to each other, in procession on the moonlit road. Soon it will be Saint John's Eve, the moon sits high in the heavens. Around the moon's disk floats strangely shaped clouds, their contours illuminated. The two nuns are talking about how Vasilika the Cripple has come home, home from the factory in Galați, because he doesn't have a job there any more, and he was talking about how on the bus he travelled on, there were other men going to the city: they babbled in a strange unintelligible tongue. And there was a woman too, with long white hair and good-sized breasts beneath her transparent shirt, because that's what women like that wear, her enormous nipples peeping out. She led the men, the white of her hair shining through the darkness. They sat down in a tavern, and by the time it had grown dark outside, they were drunk. But the problems began when, around midnight, the sleepers turned savage, kicking their beds apart, and the entire city—at least those living in the lower quarters—set off for the tavern. And the mayhem began, and you could tell it wasn't going to end well. But all this is nothing, because those evil men had already placed their feet—or rather their hooves—in that city, and in Galați too, and that's why Vasilika lost his job.

There's going to be some big trouble around here, because the Lord is not going to look upon this favourably. There might be floods, or even an earthquake . . . You know what it's like when the first cold rain begins to pelt down your throat, the muddy earth surging beneath your feet, and there's nothing for you to hold onto?

What should we do now? Sister Ankuca asks, trembling in fear.

One piece of her clothing is enough, it could even be a button, that will do. Anything that she might have touched.

Do you think it will be effective?

Of course it will.

They haggle over what item to fetch, and finally agree to bring back one of the funeral wreaths—this way, everyone can get a small part of it.

As they reach the cemetery, the nuns hear noise, and cautiously creep ahead. They see other people standing around the grave.

They got here before us, says Ankuca.

It's no problem—we'll just wait for them to leave.

Translated by Ottilie Mulzet

THE BIRTH OF EMMA K.

1

In the passport department of V. town police station, harrowed individuals wait in the windowless room referred to in the native wit as 'Auschwitz'. Upon the only chair is the snoring soldier on duty. In accordance with the new fashion, a white plastic card hangs from his jacket with the name misspelt on it in felt-tip: ISVÁN SZABÓ, the T is missing. An old couple stands in the doorway into the corridor, their daughter between them, whose name isn't brandished on her chest but I know it: Évi Ujj, she once played basketball on the school team, and was a whole head taller even than Miska Holl. Her skin is burning but there's no knowing whether it's the flea killer scattered around the room or the excitement. Her hiccups have just stopped.

The Ujj family have been planning the trip for weeks, though they didn't mention it amongst themselves so as not to jinx it. Now, capitulating in front of the dizzying possibilities, they do their best not to think. They've had plenty of practice. Not a single thought occurs, while their cerebellums tickle at the pleasure of promise. They'd go to hell and back, they just want their passports!

Neither the room's 50-watt bulbs nor the corridor's can get the upper hand. Eventually they join forces, but they'll always lose out to the coming night. Évi Ujj raises a newspaper in front of her weak eyes and softly reads but can't finish the sentence, on the far side of the room the door window unlatches, and the closed iron grate flies open.

Names fly through the air, and from all directions booming or gravelly yes's respond. After the twentieth name, Évi starts hiccupping again. She gives such a loud hiccup that the soldier wakes up but who cares now. The three names are read one after the other, at which the whole Ujj family relax. Out on the street, they've already forgotten the stuffy waiting room, though two blocks later they still stink of flea killer. At the third corner Évi brings up the paper's news story, and when they turn off at their building her mother gives the verdict: they'll postpone the journey by a day. Leftover cake from Easter, they'll cook a nice chicken soup to go with it. Yes, it's past Easter but it's still winter-coat weather. They linger a while in front of the building, somehow they don't fancy going in yet. Their minds think all sorts of nonsense. The streets are littered and a stale mustiness pours from the basement windows, but the clouds floating above the town are pretty; they'd be pretty anywhere. Not to mention the starry expanse between them. The annoying thing is the nights are still too long to spend them revelling under the frozen sky.

2

Évi cooks a better meat soup than her mother, at least her dad thinks so. They borrow a food Thermos from the neighbours because their own is awfully beat up. After searching for a long while, they find the name they're looking for in the fourth stairwell. While two stout women gather their things in the flat's poky entrance hall, the family wait in front of the door. The father, whom they call 'Pappy' amongst themselves, is getting restless. In such places, menfolk play mere supporting roles. He especially shudders at the sight of any bedridden individual, he dislikes seeing his own body in pyjamas let alone in the nip, but that's by the way. He only hopes that he's offered a cup of black coffee and a brandy. He doesn't breathe a word. Unlike his wife! They agreed not to bring up the matter but of course, he would've bet money she'd still ask. Yes indeed, all day long it's been tickling at her nose hairs! As if releasing a lusty sneeze, she softly inquires in her syrupy voice: Tell me, Mariska, dear, where's your son-in-law?

Mariska, the sister-in-law, pulls a disgusted grimace and shows them out to the kitchen, where they sit around the table in their overcoats. Pappy only begins unbuttoning once the gas is lit under the coffee pot. At every slight movement the leatherette seat cushion emits an unpleasant parp. The sister-in-law leans against the stove as she waits for the coffee, meanwhile mouthing off about the hospital conditions. She talks like a weir. Bright-red blotches shine on Pappy's face: he's allergic to razor blades, despite which he shaved yesterday and again today. He's waiting for the brandy, he'll have at least three snifters, and the wife will keep schtum. Especially now she's contemplating her own girl. Dreaming, something similar could easily happen to her, and it'd bring a lot of trouble, but after a while who remembers!

The young mother calls from the other room, and hastily turning off the gas, the sister-in-law hurries out. The family sit for a while bewildered. Pappy gets fed up and springs to his feet. He starts roughly rubbing his face. He gives his wife an accusing glare. How in God's name could she not see it!? The baby hasn't so much as peeped! He can't smell the baby, though he's particularly sensitive to it. In their time, his stomach turned at the smell of a newborn; that's when he got on the brandy. It's common knowledge that the sister-in-law isn't right in the head, so her daughter can't be either. He puffs in circles around the cramped kitchen and the women see it best to give in. Dashing out, they shout their goodbyes from the hallway, leave no money gift in the baby's shawl, and forget their Thermos too, despite giving their word they'd return it to the neighbour, who also wants to bring lunch in it to the new mother.

3

The baby, whose birth is congratulated in the paper, was a perfectly normal infant. Nor was there anything gruesome about her conception: she was the fruit of a customary, barely three-minute act. Cecília, or Cili, as she was known, had been tidying in the Vizafogó Street secondary school's science storeroom, she rolled up the maps that had been removed during the day, returned them to the cupboard, and fed the fish. She would have gone home much earlier but that morning Zakariás, the school porter, had winked at her, signalling that later when things get quiet, he'll come up, she should wait for him. She sprinkled plenty of dried water fleas into the aquarium and leaned forward to watch the fish see them off. The guppies grazed like sheep, the neon tetras went for larger lumps, standing on their heads as they gulped it down, the swordtails chased away the others first, then swam beneath the feeding ring, and the zebras floated about gormlessly. Cili pressed her forehead against the glass wall. That's when Öcsi Kovács walked in, the school's deputy caretaker, who that afternoon was going to weld a broken metal grill for the headmaster, his father-in-law-to-be. In the morning he had got the welder going, but with his boss over his shoulder hollering so many nuggets of advice, the iron simply wouldn't weld. Downstairs, in the schoolyard, he'd noticed the light on in the storeroom. Öcsi had known Cili since he was a boy, they lived on the same street. Her fragrance reminded him of paddling in the frog-filled pond, barely ten minutes from the end of the street. But it wasn't her he'd gone to the storeroom to see, it was the fish. He stood behind Cili because an open cupboard door blocked the space beside her. And then in the next minute, perhaps magnetized by the guppies' mating dance, he pressed against Cili's back. His mind was blank. As if tearing a hundred-pound sturgeon by its gills from the river that had sprawled through the school grounds before the waterways were regulated, he grabbed at her bony pelvis. Which dug into his hands, so they wandered up to her breasts. Cili, who'd been smooching the aquarium wall, started wailing. I love youuu, I love youuu! It put Öcsi off, but only a little. To tell the truth, earlier that afternoon he'd had another, much less successful act, and now liberated from that depressing memory, he was about to shout the same. But no sooner had he opened his mouth when Cili fell silent from the pleasure and just convulsed, in recurring waves, like a phone on vibrate. The storeroom's splendid wall clock, which the pupils had nicknamed the Perpetulator, struck six, but that's completely by the way.

4

At first, Öcsi Kovács wanted to marry his big sister. His plan was for them to have one single child just like him, a five-year-old. He was at school when it changed from his sister to his cousin. His cousin seemed willing too and once between the lilac bushes he showed her how he does a number one. It must have been a more complicated phenomenon than he'd expected, as some time before the jet came he felt a tingling, much to Öcsi's bewilderment. But to come back to his women matters: his beard had shot forth when he first ventured into the realms of an unknown kingdom. Which is merely a turn of phrase; he knew Zsófi Boros well. They had taken piano lessons together with Aunt Mária, a defrocked nun. The whole town respected anyone who sent their kids to Aunt Mária for piano lessons. Aunt Mária pointed out the notes with a composer's baton. Her hair was in a bun the size of a football, and it shook when the baton whacked their fingers. Or rather, the baton only ever whacked Öcsi's, because everyone spoke to little *Zsófika* like she was a precious porcelain doll, *fait main*. And Öcsi was no exception to this honey-tongued Zsófika business. At the school graduation party, they only got as far as pecking, and then they were together for six years until finally they celebrated their engagement. Both the Boros and the Kovács families had been major beneficiaries during the compensations after the regime change, and it was probably attributable to the family's past glory of one Lord Lieutenant that Mr Boros, who had been a simple history teacher in the former regime, was appointed school headmaster, despite widespread opposition among the teaching staff. Zsófi didn't get into university in the capital city but was able to graduate from a more local branch department, and Öcsi from an even more lax polytechnic, where the only care given was in collecting tuition fees. At the engagement party, Papa Boros read the following saying from a notebook with a chequered cover: 'There is in marriage a great secret, be it of the heavens, or of the earth, seek it out.' After the engagement, Zsófia announced that Öcsi would be sleeping at theirs. Papa Boros consented without much ado, what's more, welling up, he declared he wanted a grandson first, then a granddaughter, then a son again, and finally another daughter. The Kovács parents didn't go to the engagement because Öcsi forgot to tell them. Or perhaps, there was a slither of ill will in them that remained from the Lord-Lieutenant times, but that's not important.

Their lovemaking was punctilious and unsuccessful. Zsófi was never satisfied, though Öcsi tried to do everything to her wishes. Zsófi had read that if she received the seed while lying on her right side, she would have a boy.

And so for months, Emma Kovács was a boy. She wasn't called Emma but Ernő. Tamás. Márk. Miklós. Péter. Dávid. Krisztián-András-Zoltán. Rajmund. Papa Boros wanted a proper Hungarian name, Mama Boros a Catholic one. It made no difference to Öcsi. He nodded enthusiastically. Since Zsófi changed her mind from one hour to the next, whichever Öcsi had agreed to was long expired, or rather, his enduring agreement degenerated into active opposition. I don't get how anyone could have such terrible taste, derided Zsófi, her forehead burning.

Emma Kovács was an orb of an infinite radius that grew and grew. For Zsófi's name day, a friend gave her a four-week-old Pinscher puppy in a basket lined with pink silk. The whole thing fit in the palm of her hand. Through the raffia of the basket, she could feel the dog's heartbeat. The feeling entranced her and it was no coincidence that for the first few days Emma Kovács resembled a puppy. But then in the first half of June, she looked like a film star, like the one who played Spiderman. In the days after the parish fete, she looked like the infant on Mary's arm in the fresco behind the altar in Saint Anthony's. For a single hour, she waved from afar as a hardened but amicable banker. During the Saint Stephen's Day festivities, the entire historical Hungarian portrait gallery hung on the orb's walls, painted in the sombre tone of the romantic masters. The next week, they were joined by global icons, including Einstein, about whom Zsófi knew nothing beyond his portrait, and believed he was a has-been rock star.

5

Öcsi was walking home without the grill. He staggered alongside his bicycle because of a shooting pain in his crotch. He and Zsófi had been having rests after lunch too, though there was no chance of actual rest. Zsófi positioned herself on her right side and consequently, he had to lie on his left, which wasn't advised as in year nine he had suffered from heart inflammation. He had been exempt from PE class for the whole year. He lifted his right leg to forty-five degrees and kicked at the air. One-two-three-four, one-two-three-four, he repeated to himself in the gruff voice of Nyéki the PE teacher. He pretended as if this too was merely another chore, one-two-three-four, one-two-three ... He awoke to Zsófi pushing him away from herself. You finished on me again, she scolded, pushing him again so she could comfortably lie on her back, and for want of a better option, entrust the seed's delivery to gravity. But she still helped it in with a finger, and what's more, started chanting an old incantation. Little seedling, seep inside, little seedling, seep inside, Öcsi Kovács listened, and then dozed off again.

Yawning, he tramped down Vihar Street, blinking in the strong September sun. Despite there being no sign that the street's residents had been evicted and that strangers had moved into their homes: strange eyes peeked at him from behind the windows. No, they weren't strange at all but had greeted him from the shelves and glass-doored cabinets of the science storeroom countless times. The wildcat, for example, was staring from Aunt Teri's window, the long-eared owl from Nursery Teacher Manci's, the ostrich from Ferike Semsey's, and the lynx from the Gózners'. On Kölcsey's corner, the town's solitary traffic light, which had slowly changed from red to green since his childhood, reminded him of Gonzo, the now one-eyed orangutan. Pallay had prised out the other eye and traded it for a silver pengő coin with Franz Joseph's face on it. Two-thirds of the way up the street, opposite the cobbler's, stood the crucifix, since the times when it marked the town limits. Looking at Christ's green eyes, it seemed he wanted to say something. For Öcsi, this message was undoubtedly: just four more houses until home. A bird was cowering on top of the stone cross. It closed its eyes like a conceited, forlorn writer: when the world praises the latest sensation, he just shrugs, he wrote that one ages ago! But I can say without a drop of conceit: I know the bird's name. Everyone called him Jókai. Truth be told, there wasn't a great number of birds in the town since the general secretary's visit sometime in the early seventies, when Kálmán Nyéki dyed them all red with permanent aniline. At the time red was the colour of loyalty. Nevertheless, the birds fled, while the behaviour of those that remained displayed a combination of aggression and confusion. Zakariás could say, given the number of times he'd had to call the glazier because there was a window in the school, on the Vizafogó Street side, on the first floor, beside the drain pipe, which received monthly kamikaze attacks.

Öcsi Kovács could have found his way home from school with his eyes closed. It was like he was being reeled home by a thin strand of wet, glistening paste. Yet really, there was no small amount of danger around. Though in V. accidents were rare, were we to enlarge the town, keeping its proportions, to just a middle-sized town, the number would soar terrifically. Among the slates of the Uszkais' house, at least three were ready to come crashing down, not to mention Old Aunt Surányi's shack: one of the walls could collapse at the faintest tremor. That very afternoon, at least three car users were driving drunk, one of whom ended up in the riverbed, having broken through the barrier on Várdomb Street. They could have knocked down Öcsi, too. At the same time, we mustn't forget the human body's internal disasters. It wouldn't have been implausible, after all, it had been a tiring day, for a vein to pop in his brain or his heart to stop. What's more, we can't say there was zero chance of a meteor crashing down on his head. Ultimately, nor can we exclude street activity and spontaneous demonstrations: an unpredictable crowd can beat even the most innocent passers-by to a pulp. Were I not following Öcsi's route from below, but from above, from an orbiting space station, I could report back on this labyrinth, littered with obstacles, crossroads, and snares, in which a safe arrival was much less probable than might be understood, judging by V.'s scale.

Since it was still light out, he pushed his bicycle into the woodshed, and without saying hello to his parents who were already in front of the TV, he climbed the cherry tree, and into his snug, self-constructed nest. The sparrows started chirping under the eaves. He took down his slingshot, dug out a pebble from a food can, and shot it at the drainpipe. The tin tube pinged, and then quiet.

Overhead, the sky cleared like an enormous projector screen. The light poured upwards, leaving the depths of the gardens in darkness. Blinding flashes circled the sky, laughing and raging. They couldn't find a single cloud where they could settle, and so they scorched the rising specks of dust with their kisses. Öcsi longed for the same: upwards, the roof of the sky. For twenty years he had kneaded his fantasies, and every time he jumped from the tree, hope pulsed through him, that he'd start floating, slowly and solemnly plunging into the sky's depths. Forever thinking about inventions, he imagined that he ought to charge himself electrostatically. He closed his eyes, poked his index finger beyond the cherry tree's perfect sphere, and taking deep breaths, pictured himself being touched by a huge ebonite rod, at which, like a scrap of paper, he would start floating skywards.

The smell of cabbage pasta swirled around the yard, Öcsi's stomach gave a loud rumble, and his eyes popped open. Reflected in his eyes, replacing the wandering specks of dust, were twinkling astral phenomena. Anyone who has lived in a small town on a plain knows how many of them fit onto the far-reaching sky. The Plough Öcsi called the Goose, and the Seven Sisters the Wart. What's known on a star chart as the Little Bear was the Water Spider, Cassiopeia he knew as Little Eight. He visited Lyra's every star one after another with his extendable telescope. He named them off: Spring Rain, Wildflower, Teardrop, Worm, Mole Ear, Swiss Hunter. When he was in a good mood, he gave out names without stopping, and the next day he remembered every last one.

He grabbed a horizontal branch, swung out, and swept forward. For a single minute, hanging above the darkness, he felt as though the Earth's power had weakened and just this once would let him go. But so much daydreaming was a lot for one day, and his arms growing weak too, he thudded to the ground.

And as his feet thudded, in that very moment, in a negative explosion, Emma Kovács's orb of an infinite radius shrank to two millimicrons.

6

The moment of the orb's implosion was immediately followed by a positive explosion. The name of this new, expanding orb was none other than hunger. The two-nanometre-wide Emma K. was gripped by the eating frenzy and gobbled down everything within reach. Drunk with joy, she saw how easily she could meet new companions, and how easily she could come to an agreement with them in this wild feeding. At a dizzying pace, they twisted and joined the new plumbing, laid the new pipes, and hollowed out mouths and stomachs. The workers were united by an understanding of the highest order, a noble solidarity, as if moving to one melody. Nobody knew the plan, yet the two arms, triumphs of meticulous design, grew on either side, for seizing nourishment, the two legs shot forth, for deliverance to fresh pastures, and the brains bubbled, for concocting the most ticklish flavours that inject new fluids into the slowing stomach. Emma K. wanted the infinite radius back, not a centimetre less.

By the time Öcsi had eaten the second plate of cabbage pasta, Emma K., stretching well beyond expectations, had swollen to the size of an ant egg, while her form most resembled the nuggets that Öcsi had picked from his nose in his snug nest, flicking them by the dozen into the air. By the time Öcsi had drunk his mint tea, brushed his teeth and lain down, the ant egg had rolled to her new home and was getting accustomed to its unusual climate; she wet herself with excitement when a stranger whom she had bitten, not only didn't reject her advances but warmly opened an umbrella over her head.

7

Öcsi Kovács's former friends would have been ashamed to return to the world of slingshot pinging, button flicking, butterfly catching, and tree climbing. What would their kids say when they couldn't flick a ten-pointer button two metres? Or when instead of whacking the pige stick out of the yard, they fluffed it entirely? Nor did Öcsi have any new friends, so nobody knew that he hunkered at home all day. In fact, Zsófi didn't miss him either. She didn't even notice that he hadn't called in for weeks.

He spent the warm, honey-coloured autumn afternoons in his nest and studied the lives of the newest generation of swallows through his telescope. He returned to who he had been before Zsófi had ever set her sights on him.

In the last days of October, the weather cooled. The leaves turned yellow and they fell in a single night. November arrived with hoarfrost and rime. The long-awaited, abundant autumn rainfall didn't come and the frozen ground was as hard as a block of wood. The Kovács family were preparing to visit the graveyard for All Saints' Day. At this time of year, Öcsi's older sister came home from the other end of the country, where she worked as a geologist at a mining firm with her husband. In the last year, she'd doubled in weight because she'd been given office work and wasn't working onsite.

Öcsi Kovács loved to stare at the candles flickering by the gravestones and collected the strange shapes of the dripping wax in matchboxes. His gaze would rest on the homemade lanterns that protected the shivering flames from the wind.

His family were solemnly getting ready for the afternoon excursion, but entirely unbeknownst to him. Only when they were leaving, squeezing into the Skoda, did his father call over to him sinisterly, he doesn't deserve to come, why should they bring him. To which he asked, why he was saying that, and his father replied, he knows very well why.

They stood around the grave in silence. After a short while, the brother-in-law went to visit his own relatives' graves, and they were left alone. That's when his mother started. Staring daggers at Öcsi, she hissed: how's Cili? Öcsi didn't understand the question and then of course the penny immediately dropped. How should I know, he replied automatically. His mother's face began to quietly rage. He knew this phase well, or the wrath that was to come, no wonder he gave an entreating glance to his older sister, and then his father. He could always count on his father, who usually maintained his neutrality and sooner or later came around to Öcsi's side. Now, however, he was furrowing his brow reproachfully, and seemingly unable to wait for the denouement of this scene that had only begun, it shot out like a bullet: you good for nothing! Öcsi's mother, furious that her husband had jumped ahead, now ploughed on, gasping for air, almost incoherent, as she scattered attributives for that filthy, slutty, crackpot of a little tart.

Trollop, the sister chimed in. It was the first time Öcsi had heard this word; its meaning, however, he could read from her face. Though he still tried raising his eyebrows as if puzzled, because he often found that his sister forgot to box him across the ears when she could gloatingly explain something to him. Trollop, stupid hussy, zipper on her knickers, went on their mother.

Öcsi Kovács stood with his head bowed, trapped between the graves. He shrank. He was shocked by the news which he too had suspected for at least two weeks. Cili had been constantly hanging around. She came down to the workshop a few times, and when he escaped which he always did, she sent after him a typical movement with her hand, as if caressing an imaginary bump. Of course, even if not consciously, the message was received somewhere in his brain. Why did he have to go to the school that afternoon? If it hadn't been for that grill, or if Zsófi had left him in peace, or if the light hadn't been on, or if he hadn't looked up, or if Zakariás had bolted the gate . . . The heavy sand of two weeks' self-delusion came crashing down on him. He had hoped that nothing had happened, that the mild summer evenings would last forever.

From among the graves, he saw the gravel path where an old woman dressed in black, tipping her body from one foot to the other, slowly creaked towards them. He shivered because he felt naked. Cili's belly is like an X-ray machine . . . He's standing there before probing eyes, vainly trying to cover his crotch though the wind is patting his backside, his stained pyjamas hanging in his hands, convulsively crumpling them, the unsettling whiff in his nostrils that his parents, perhaps even the neighbours, can smell. He was dripping with sweat. He shuddered in the buffeting icy wind. He hoped he'd have a fever by the evening and he could go to bed. But that wouldn't work either because his mother would sit with him, nursing him, and her piercing eyes would see straight through him. He could keep nothing secret from her. She knew everything yet she'd still scourge him to tell her. So much for the usual atmosphere of All Saints' Day. His vain dreams of candles . . . The wind whistled eerily through crosses welded together from iron pipes. If only the earth would swallow him up! Maybe if a sod of earth shifted beneath him it'd solve his situation. But everywhere was concrete, meticulously swept with a feather duster. The handles on the covering slab were so rusted that not even an iron grip could budge it. It's interesting, it suddenly occurred to him, his family never mention the dead. At most the state of the grave, the cemetery wardens' work, and the quality of the wreath; not a word about the grave's inhabitants.

His mother fell silent, then asked a question he couldn't answer of course, but at least she let him speak.

How many months is she?

Where are you getting this from?

Come on, son, even the sparrows are twittering.

It was a saying of hers and when she said it, especially with the word 'twittering', he could be sure his mother was no longer angry. She can't be many, she answered for him. There was no more anger in her tone, she became pensive as if thinking about something else. From here on in is a more favourable phase, the wheels are in motion and begin grinding for the flour-paste solution.

The usual family council was in session, everyone brought something to the table and threw in ideas that might bring them closer to a solution to their shared problem. They successfully resolved murky and complex questions, because if they didn't immediately come to a tangible result, they sidestepped lethargy, then took another step and examined things from a new angle. When his grandmother had got cancer and they all knew there was nothing to be done, they still managed to push through the deadlock and convinced his grandmother to go for an operation, which made no sense, looking back. But then the funeral went without a hitch, at the feast even Öcsi got a glass of brandy. By the time Öcsi's brother-in-law came back, the scowling was over; they cheerfully rattled on home.

8

Cili came for 6 p.m., that's all Öcsi had told her over the phone. She'd seen his mother before, a proud woman, who held her back straight, even when picking through spuds at the market. His mother didn't fuss over introductions and reached straight for the girl's belly.

Cili had washed her hair with the nettle shampoo she'd got from Zakariás for Christmas. Normally she used soap. She wore her bally cardigan with the puffy sleeves. Below she was wearing her lace black knickers, prepared for anything. And she was right. She had even applied eyeliner.

Öcsi's mother tugged up the white blouse under her cardigan and shoved her hot hand between the skirt and the hem of her underwear. It's soft, she said to her daughter, who had stayed a few days because work at the mining firm had stopped due to some accident and only her husband had to go back. Have a feel!

No, it's not soft, said Öcsi's sister, as her hand joined her mother's under the cardigan. It's completely hard here.

Cili patted her belly and nodded.

Soon Öcsi's mother found the spot, her hand froze and her face grew serious. It's hard, she nodded darkly. Cili unbuttoned her cardigan and lowered her underwear so they could reach her belly more easily. Öcsi's father too, who, after being forced to cut short his studies at the technical university, had become a seller at the porcelain section of Vasudvar Department Store, and had both a good eye for the wares and a real panache for the buyers' language, that is, he knew how to handle people. He convinced the stubbornest shopper that the cracked jug is a bargain, and in fact, that little crack's a mere scratch, it'll wear off with use. He didn't even need to touch her belly, he could see how hard it was.

Indeed, in Cili's belly, Emma K. was now bigger than a pea. She looked like three egg-barley pellets stuck together, one big one, and two little ones. Seemingly sensing their curious gaze, she threw out her chest. It was intoxicating, day by day life grew more intoxicating for her. The ancient orb of an infinite radius hadn't collapsed completely, its memory quivered in the ether, or rather, its traces were retained in the vibrational frequency of the ether's every particle.

Many, many hours follow the 6 p.m. shown on the face of the Perpetulator, likely tens of thousands, when one fine day Emma K. hears these vibrations with her own ears. A man whispers something to her, and in the whisper, in the aniseed-scented breath, which has caused her clothes to drop more than once, she discovers that the orb of an infinite radius exists. What an evening that is! Its sky purple with mindless happiness, so much, a horn ought to be blown for people to come with buckets, with quilts, to take some home, there's plenty for everyone. In the morning she wasn't in love, or at noon, but by the evening she is. She doesn't understand. For days there's only dazzling light, she sees neither day nor night. She spends the nighttimes filling four notebooks. The next morning she can barely read the words. She's getting nowhere with the story, though it's more realistic, horrifying, glittering, cogent and cryptic than the rest. Oh, someone else will write it!

Once again the three pellets of egg barley widdled with excitement. And for a moment, relaxed before quickly tensing. The skin on Cili's tummy twitched. There, poked Öcsi's mother, without holding back, instead slamming her finger into the skin.

It has to soften, it'll cling on as long as it's hard!

The kitchen table was the father's idea, who helped Cili up from the stool, and then up from the floor. And he felt her first. She should lift something heavy, said Öcsi's mother.

Öcsi Kovács hadn't a single useful suggestion. He was ashamed for being so useless, after all, he should be taking the lead. His sister, though! She was pretty well informed on the subject matter and now he could see just how well. The divan was her suggestion because Cili could just reach under it, it's easy to get a grip of, and if someone sits on it, it'll be heavier depending on where they sit. Finally, Öcsi could make himself useful. He devised that he would jump on the bed to produce a jolting undulation, the kind that topples even bridges. But his father talked him out of it, lest he ruin the springs. The point is: exertion, barked the sister, get her sweating.

Cili grunted loudly, so they could see the effort. Her face went completely red, after a while a slow fluid began flowing down her thighs, and she got scared. It was just the sweat dripping off her back; no result yet. Öcsi's mother threw in the next idea, that they need a more direct, more precise impact, that'd hit exactly the right spot. She knew what she wanted, of course, but she didn't want to go first. Her daughter understood, told Cili to lift her clothes, made a fist, pointing the knuckle of her middle finger, and gave her a lightning-fast jab.

For the whole evening, their patience held out. If they did start getting on each other's nerves, it was merely because they had the same goal, the desire to achieve it was shared and everyone wanted to demonstrate that they would do everything in their power to succeed. And Cili was sucked into this whirlpool too, happily battering her own belly. Her fist bounced off it, comically, like punching a football. At that point, Öcsi's father, fed up with their inaccuracy, boxed her in the gut, with calculated precision and all the strength he could muster. Cili doubled over, for a second even lost consciousness, dropped to her knees, but then lifted her head to indicate she was all right, in fact, maybe now . . . Yes, yes, it's softer, and laughed, through irrepressible, welling tears, and revealing her terrible teeth. Öcsi's mother eagerly grabbed her. The others watched. No, no, it hasn't, came the verdict. A frightened shadow came over Cili's face, but she willingly lifted her crumpled clothes and turned her tummy back to the department-store salesman.

Öcsi Kovács teetered beside the kitchen table ever more nervously. As well as he tried to shoo away the image, he vividly remembered the time his father had furiously taken apart the propeller aeroplane Öcsi had assembled from the sewing machine, with—for an eleven-year-old—the precision of an engineer and the ingenuity of a true craftsman, on which his father even commented. It troubled him that again they were ruining something that was his concern. He became irate at his father, who always wanted to be the master handyman when in reality he was incapable of fixing the most basic appliances. And his eyesight was no good any more. His aim was lazy. So, beating his father to it, he angrily thumped Cili one himself because he saw they ought to be aiming at least two inches lower. Öcsi aimed two inches lower and hit his mark. This time Cili did faint. They nervously splashed water on her face, sat her on the couch, Öcsi's sister offered her some brandy, and they got her a cup of tea. They agreed to continue the next day. But until then, Öcsi's mother recommended mustard-seed tea and a scalding hot bath. Do you have a bath? Tap water isn't hot enough, add boiled water from the stove. And tomorrow, come after dark.

9

When so intoxicated with joy, Emma K. always ended up musing over philosophical thoughts. She imagined that loving care evenly dispersed about the world smothers its goodness upon everything within reach. Or rather, no sooner does a being present themselves to that loving care, than that being becomes 'within reach'. She was completely drunk on the attention she was being paid. And then at the first punch, she saw stars. She didn't understand how they'd reappeared: they had once glimmered on the walls of the orb of an infinite radius. Unsurprisingly, she was immediately brushed by the soft butterfly wings of hope, look, little girl, you've got what you've been looking for, you've got your orb back. Yet a moment later, darkness replaced the stars and the three egg-barley pellets twitched in pain's icy dirt. Cells that had bound with secret whispers of desire and noble silvery threads of agreement wanted to scatter with near-prodigal negligence. What had come together in delicate balance would be lost to the world. Past entered present, and future enveloped the ancestral. Emma K. looked like Jókai the Bird, cowering on the cross, feet growing from its tousled back, and when it flew it seemed to flap belly up, tail first. Matter had broken down and time with it. God, Himself couldn't have found his bearings in this chaos. Though I knew the bird's name, there's no chance I could see inside Emma K.'s head, too. I can only guess at what she pictured.

In any case, she was standing in front of a horse, opposite what used to be the cobbler's on Vihar Street with her back to the cross. The horse was lying on the road. Now and again it lifted its head. No, at first it was still standing. Beside it was a cart and around the cart were logs of wood. A bristly man who smelled like a brewery was beating the horse with a stick as thick as his arm. The figures present in the scene show how time has stopped in V.: people are still burning wood in their homes and using horse-drawn carts on the streets. The one change in the picture is the Internet Cafe where the cobbler's used to be. The carter walloped the horse's head again and again. The horse's eyes swam in blood but the eyeballs were bulging from the crimson puddles and looking straight at Emma Kovács. Who else could they have been looking at? Aunt Terike was standing there but just laughed. Uncle Pityu Gózner too. And Dezső Kodra laughed as he greeted her, hi, little Emma, not skipping school I hope! His wife beside him, Aunt Ica Kodra, who was also far from cold sober, of course, but still wore a friendly smile; when she really was full as a · goat, she went to class and with her frail hands was known to slap Túróczi or Juli Kádas until she drew blood. Emma's namesake, Enikő Kovács, or Kovieni, was laughing too. Truth be told, Emma K. never had a strong sense of humour. She watched numbly as the brewery-smelling, panting man dealt the horse whack after whack to the head; his smock coat, grimy with dirt, swishing dreadfully with every blow . . . Goddamn fucking animal! he shouted. Emma K. was no churchgoer, nor did she pray but the words sent an icy bolt right through her. She covered her ears. She didn't want to cover her eyes because she was worried the next blow would fall on her. She should've walked on but she couldn't bear to move. She had no idea how this day would end. Will she make it home at all? And then she grew used to the spectacle, what's more, she started to be angry; if the horse can bear the harshest blows, doesn't kick, doesn't bite, doesn't run off, then with the same strength, why not obey, why not do whatever it is that will sedate this lager-breathed man's fit of rage? And though she arrived home not long after because a passing neighbour took her by the hand and brought her home, the story lasted all evening, all night and all the next day too. Until this very moment. The question remains, if the horse can't bear to kick back or run off, then why not die? That was the most horrifying part. Why doesn't it croak?

The second punch was unexpected too, and the third. She expected the fourth. What on earth! she started, and clenched her teeth, that is, she clung on with unyielding resolve. She did nothing unusual, she hadn't any sort of strategy. Maybe it wasn't even her, but what had formed from the desire to recover the orb of an infinite radius, yes, the rage, the stubborn rage built in her into a concrete pillar: she threw her arms around it. Were a grown-up to hold their breath for two minutes, they'd begin to understand the sincerity of Emma K.'s determination. How long is two minutes? Eight pendulum swings of the Perpetulator or an average-length sentence. It wasn't the beating that was the most testing, she almost enjoyed that, but the aftereffect that drew energy from the surrounding, flexible walls and strengthened the force of the waves, so that the resonance penetrated the deep with self-destructive triumph, like a swollen spring tide, capable of throwing all the waters of the ocean onto the shore.

10

Zsófi first thought of Öcsi weeks later, when she heard of Cili's condition. Choked with rage, she stamped her feet until she felt sick. And as she was heaving over the toilet, suddenly, like a soap bubble, a thought filled with colour: the real reason she's feeling sick can be nothing other than the longed-for pregnancy. She could feel her belly was larger than usual. Her breasts too. And look, there was a drop of milk on her nipple. Thinking back, she'd missed a few months now.

A gold bracelet sparkled on the wrist of the gynaecologist, Gábor Bátori, who had a respectable name. He had come into his surgery the day after Christmas for Zsófi. He'd waited for her excitedly since the morning. He's Jewish, Zsófi's mother had once told her in a low voice as if telling her of a sore hidden under her clothes. Though Zsófi had never been forbidden from speaking to him, her mother's tone and expression deterred her. But Gábor did his best to charm her, and actually, she also spent the school basketball games staring at the slender boy's body under the backboard. It was probably for Zsófi that Gábor became a gynaecologist. Is there no end to the fantasies of a rejected lover?!

He veiled his embarrassment with pompous jargon. Medical science achieved its greatest successes in its study of the female body. It was an incontrovertible fact that achievements in studying the human hormonal system were made via studying the secretory products of the female organism. When Zsófi took off her underwear and stepped behind the folding screen, Gábor, left alone with the shiny blue knickers, couldn't resist the temptation, with one twitch of the pituitary gland the inebriating hormone shot like a black arrow into his sexual glands, causing even his closely cropped hair to stand: trembling, he lowered his head and brushed his lips against the silk lacing. Almost fainting from the smell, the timbre of his tremor reached its apex. He stood a while, looking at the ceiling, and concentrated his attention on one of the lamp's missing screws. He sighed, stepped behind the folding screen, mechanically spread some kind of white ketchup on Zsófi's belly and applied the head of the ultrasound scanner.

Long minutes passed. The deep and heavy smell washed out the gluey alluvium from deeper and deeper in Gábor's brain. A stirring, wild, fearless smell! He was bowled over but he didn't mind, he'd happily be its eternal slave. If only he was . . .

You could give birth as early as tomorrow. You've begun dilating. I'll check the cervix but I can already make out the thickness with the ultrasound. The internal orifice has almost disappeared. The glands of the fallopian tubes are squelching with the anticipation and the muscles of the pelvic floor have stretched. I'm amazed you aren't having contractions. I can see the perineum has thickened. Forget tomorrow, you could give birth now, any minute. Except. There's nothing there. It's a false pregnancy. As if you really wanted to. Or you're really scared to.

I really want to. I want to!

Gábor Bátori took another cowardly timeout behind the screen, staggered to his desk, rummaged among the files, then returned and awkwardly collapsed onto Zsófi, buried his face in her, and inhaled, inhaled her smell. I can help, he croaked.

Zsófi didn't dare to sleep for two days because when she did she saw Gábor's face appear between her thighs like she was giving birth to him. She regretted going to see him and felt ashamed, or rather teenage disgust. She despised herself. She showered every two hours. Finally, on the afternoon of the last New Year's Eve of the Millenium, she was relieved to discover that her period had come. She stared through tears at the pink drops dripping into the bathtub. Before loudly declaring: No mercy. I'll get Öcsi Kovács fired, there's no doubt about that. And as long as I live, I'll be after his bastard child.

11

Emma K. noticed she had a new orb. One that shone a painful neon blue. She had no experience to compare the pain to, yet was sure she was suffering the absolute worst.

After a blow harder than hard, it occurred to her the best solution was to disappear. If everything fell to bits the pain would disappear too. She made a decision, she wouldn't hold on, wouldn't contract, wouldn't stiffen, she would let herself be pummelled like the horse. But inside her, the enraged, tenacious matter wouldn't let her: it kept kicking back.

And there was something else too. Through the pain's menacing numbness, she felt the warmth of the hand that had led her home from the horse-beating carter; she could feel the palm's warm silk. And then there was an open pair of palms, into which someone buried their face, then bending over, they cried out that they'd give anything, they'd give their life, in return for hers.

Next, there were distant beings who nervously watched every time her condition turned for the worse and the threads balefully snapped. Curiously, they had the same face, her own shrivelled, shapeless, incomplete face. The giant head of a nestling dove, a revived little hammer. And as for how far the effect of the connections' dynamic reached, just look to the forests of Japan and the macaques' uneasiness. It is said that these primates were once humans, then became animals but that a godlike perspicacity still resides within them. When Emma K. was in trouble and headed towards self-annihilation, they unearthed a secret resource from which they pumped her the necessary energy. The matter within Emma K. kicked back and anti-venoms were produced to choke the injected serpents. Her muscles coiled around the pillar of fortitude like wiry monkey arms. A while later, she had regained such strength that she slammed even the slightest violation, rebutting the gentlest brush with furious delight.

12

Two months passed. Then another two, during which matters were put to rest; nor did the orb of pain grow. One thought arose that's worthy of mention, an inkling. Emma K. rightly suspected she might have something to do with this calm. Perhaps it wasn't her stubbornness that had won but something else. But what? She can't see it in the mirror though it's written on her face. When she reaches for it, it slips away, and when she does catch it, it immediately transforms. It quenches no thirst and soothes no hunger, yet she thirsts for it and hungers for it.

And then, what had been absent for two months came back in one fell swoop. It caught her off guard and was horrific. The light flaring in her eyes was horrific. With primordial strength, an immense force seized her, tore her from the pillar of stubbornness like a tatty slip of paper, and flung her face forward onto her nose. It was horrific and yet she had never felt such relief. Maybe that was when she first felt at home with the word *primordial*. There are words that never become fully integrated. They have meaning of course but what's important is their music. Were we to gather them from the vast array of languages, we could describe the world's primeval state. *Promise* is a lovely word, but *cauliflower ears* and *Schurkenstreich* are just as lovely to those who can hear in them the echoing sounds of eternity.

From that moment on, Emma K. felt at home on whatever road an immense force swept her down. And so she felt at home on Vihar Street, with its unique silvery weave. Then on another street with another house. On the avenue down which a milky white taxi races her to the hospital. On the staircase whose steps she tries to count but gets confused. In the cruelly narrow corridor through which she's ushered into a brightly lit room. She could have strolled the roads to the depths of hell and the flowery meadows of heaven like she'd walked them all before. If her life map had become indecipherable with a mess of tiny dashes, these glowing straight lines burned through the paper.

Naturally, she also knew the road that led from this life back to the orb of an infinite radius. She knew it well. But that's all by the way.

Finally, she thought, and welled with burning tears. Finally, it's all becoming clear.

She had learnt all that she could know. Nothing's fine. Being a thing of the world's matter is worth too little. Others may vainly sing its praises but she won't. The problem is in matter! In the marvelled-at laws. In gravity, in causality, in interrelationship, there's no good to be found. Transformation comes with annihilation, annihilation with pain. The worm is buried deep within the laws. That one and one make two is bad. That electricity is induced in an electromagnetic field is bad. That carbon and silicon atoms burn the most violently while others merely flicker on tiptoes is bad. That the smallest grain of dust behaves the same as the biggest is bad. That the whole world is the same is bad. That we can't move to another because the world lets nobody leave is bad. Once a prisoner, always a prisoner.

Suddenly her skull was jammed, it had got stuck. She started to struggle. She felt a painful blow, this time from within. Perhaps it was her beating heart. She froze and plunged deeper, or rather realized she'd been struggling in the wrong direction, and when she relaxed, she slid easily. This last easing off unleashed more waves of crying. She hiccupped, blubbered, and growled like an angry young marmot. The midwives, flocking from all directions, huddled together and peeked inside, terrified, to glimpse what monstrosity was to come, each of them ready to take flight if there was trouble. On that day Gábor Bátori happened to be the doctor on duty, but as to why he was missing, that's for another story. Oh God, oh God, screamed Cili, and at the sound of the word, the room expanded and deepened outwards towards the ceiling, as though a real sky yawned overhead. And in this vastness the pain that was forcing her thighs open though she wanted to close them diminished. But she still couldn't because she was tied down. The only way is open! She shuddered, as though coming . . . Emma K. feels the situation lighten too. No longer is she being dragged by that force and yet simply remembering it for a moment, just the memory would turf her out. Such a horrific light! Her body stiffens, she can't move her arms or legs, the crying catches in her chest but her soul demands its denied right. She drops like a cobblestone, almost into the dirty bucket. Only when a hand pats her back and dapples her with cold water does the compressed air whoosh from her with a mixture of tears, vomit, snot, dirt, and blood. So fiercely she sprays even those at the far side. For a moment the atmosphere numbs, like in a cosy room when a stranger bursts in. Got her, says the midwife, holding her. Her body seizes with another cramp. Her mouth is open but she isn't breathing. She looks as if she's smiling. She has control over her own will. She can send commands to her muscles. She's likely never felt so victorious and never will, because now and now only she holds her fate in her own two hands. All she has to do is not take a breath. She subjects her lungs to her control . . . She forces her muscles to obey . . . However much her body protests, she'll do it gladly. She's so dazed with joy, she's barely able to appreciate her sight returning to dark. And then even more elated, she glimpses the new brilliance of that darkness. She came into this world to turn back, torching her pointless experience of delivery in the nearing brilliance. The light is horrifying and the dark's brilliance is intoxicating. There's no knowing what's on the other side. Something. When a blow harder than hard had turfed her out, she was nowhere to be found. But she must have been somewhere because when she returned she remembered being nowhere. Now she can find out. Maybe another story exists in which she returns another time. So long, Emma K.!

In a moment as short as resolve, a sound gushes into her ears. From the neighbouring birthing chair, they unfasten the other mother who was in labour at the same time and momentarily lay her red baby on her gasping belly. They stick a plaster on the infant's wrist and write his name in indelible pencil, Lázár Szabó, who starts crying from all the fuss and bother with an orphan's abandon. His mother's touch lends no comfort. As if planted on the chest of his killer, his desperation peaks. In these sounds, Emma Kovács recognizes the orb of the wicked and infinite void. And without knowing why, her hands twitch, her tensed muscles relax, light trickles into her pupils, she takes a breath: she joins in the song. She pities the crying baby, she pities his crying, deathly-pale mother, she pities her own mother, she pities the midwives. Her cry is a single wail but floods from her like a pulsating aria that leaves the audience stock still. The labour ward falls silent. The warm rain of true relief begins to fall, the arms and thighs relax, and a soothing shiver strokes the lengths of their wet spines.

Translated by Owen Good